A DREAM TO BELIEVE IN

KAY CORRELL

ROSE QUARTZ PRESS

Published by Rose Quartz Press

011519/071220

Strange as it may seem, this book is dedicated to the Rocky Mountains. I went to camp in the Rockies each summer. That experience was a transformative part of my childhood. It gave me my life-long love of the mountains and taught me so much about life, self-discovery, friendship, and the beauty and power of nature.

story between series - with Josephine and Paul from The Letter.)

LIGHTHOUSE POINT ~ THE SERIES
Wish Upon a Shell - Book One
Wedding on the Beach - Book Two
Love at the Lighthouse - Book Three
Cottage near the Point - Book Four
Return to the Island - Book Five
Bungalow by the Bay - Book Six

CHARMING INN ~ Return to Lighthouse Point
One Simple Wish - Book One
Two of a Kind - Book Two
Three Little Things - Book Three
Four Short Weeks - Book Four
Five Years or So - Book Five
Six Hours Away - Book Six

SWEET RIVER ~ THE SERIES
A Dream to Believe in - Book One
A Memory to Cherish - Book Two
A Song to Remember - Book Three
A Time to Forgive - Book Four
A Summer of Secrets - Book Five
A Moment in the Moonlight - Book Six

CHAPTER 1

Nora Cassidy slipped out the door of her cabin at Sweet River Lodge. The sun poked over the mountain peaks in the distance, coating the sky with a pale pink burst of watercolor. She sucked in a deep breath of the fresh piney air. The light breeze was crisp and cool against her cheeks. This was her heaven on earth. Her favorite spot on the planet. The faint drone of an engine in the distance caught her attention. No doubt her early-riser son clearing the road of the light dusting from last night's gentle snowfall.

She tugged on her gloves and started down the pathway along the stream. The water rushed over the rocks with a riotous force from the recent melting spring snow, not that she thought that last night's fresh snow was the last they'd see this spring. She hurried to the main lodge. Miss Judy would be making cinnamon rolls, and there was a hot mug of coffee waiting with her name on it. She needed to go to her office and see what all needed to be done today. There was always a long list of to-dos at the lodge, but she didn't mind the hard work. She loved Sweet River Lodge and everything about it. Things had slowed down a bit after the holiday rush. It gave her time to catch up and take a bit of time to herself.

Well, she always *said* she'd take some time for herself but rarely managed to make that happen. Except for her twice-weekly trek into town to have coffee or lunch with Annie. That was something she seldom skipped.

She looked up at the sky as it brightened into an azure blue.

This.

This was the perfect life. She felt sorry for anyone who wasn't her today. She whistled under her breath as she hurried into the lodge to make sure everything was ready for the breakfast crowd.

ANNIE DAVENPORT HURRIED along Main Street in Sweet River Falls, a worn backpack slung over one shoulder. She'd carted the laptop home last night to work on accounting, a boring but necessary job. She was trying her best to juggle the accounts to help pay for the remodel of what had been unused loft space to expand her shop. She'd finally been approved for a loan, which worried her a bit because she didn't like to owe money to anyone. But it was an unavoidable business decision she'd made.

Soon Bookish Cafe would be twice the size, giving her room to expand the coffee shop area, set up a larger internet lounge for the many people who couldn't get internet at their mountain homes, and room for a dedicated children's reading area for the bookstore.

So many plans. So little time. She could hear her best friend Nora's voice in her head. Nora always teased her about her big plans. Not that Nora didn't have her own plans for the lodge. She was always adding on and improving it, trying to make it a profitable business that her son would one day take over.

She snatched the keys from her pocket and unlocked the front door. The shop would open in thirty minutes. Time to get the coffee made and the shades opened up to the pretty view of Sweet River out the back of the shop.

She crossed to her office and snatched off her knitted hat, mindlessly running her fingers through her short blonde hair in an effort to calm it from the resulting riotous mess. She hung her parka on a hook, tugged off her boots, and slipped on a pair of simple flats from the backpack.

She walked out into the shop and pulled open the blinds. The stream behind the shop gurgled its way down the mountain, rushing over the smooth, tumbled rocks. Before long there would be sunny days when it would be warm enough to sit outside on the patio by the river. The town had put in a pathway that ran behind all the shops along the river. Once it warmed up, the path would be filled with people strolling by and hopefully stopping in for coffee, a sandwich, or to browse through the bookstore. Her shop had become a friendly gathering place for the townsfolk as well as a busy spot for visitors during the tourist season.

She smiled as she set about starting coffee with her special blend of coffee beans. She loved living in Sweet River Falls. She was one lucky woman. She had everything she needed. This was the perfect place to live, and she couldn't imagine ever leaving.

NICK CHAMBERS HAD FORGOTTEN how crisp the Colorado air could be. Crisp and *clean*. Not like the smoggy air in Los Angeles. He drew in a deep breath and pulled his too-light-for-this-weather jacket tightly around him. He looked up and down the street until he found the store he was looking for. Alpine Outfitters. He hurried down the sidewalk in his totally inappropriate leather dress shoes and slipped in the door of the shop.

An hour later he re-emerged dressed in jeans, boots, a winter parka, and a decent pair of gloves. The bag he carried held a pair of cowboy boots. He hadn't had a pair in over thirty years and hadn't been able to resist. Another bag held flannel shirts, more jeans, and a couple of sweaters. His California wardrobe wasn't going to cut it out here.

He stopped at the SUV he'd rented and tossed the bags into the backseat. He looked at the paper he'd grabbed listing off places to rent. For now, he'd gotten a room at a motel on the edge of town, but he really didn't want to spend two-plus months in a motel room. He'd go check out some short-term rentals in the next few days after he figured out what his schedule would be. He paused again, looking up at the snowcapped mountains in the distance. The sun shone brightly on the snow-laden branches of the trees. It almost looked like a picture-perfect postcard.

Did people send postcards anymore? He grinned at the thought.

Suddenly, he was sure he'd made the right decision to take this temporary teaching position at Mountain Grove College. They'd asked him to fill in for a professor who'd been injured in a skiing accident. Nick figured a couple months of teaching would be a welcome break, and he'd requested a leave from his position in Los Angeles. He'd been a bit worried about returning to his home state, but now, after being here for only a few hours, he knew in his bones that this was what he needed right now. A place he could heal.

CHAPTER 2

Nora pushed through the door to Bookish Cafe. Annie waved to her and sent her a just-a-minute sign. She wandered over to stand by the windows and looked out at Sweet River. The town had cleared the snow from the pathway behind the shops, and a lone couple strolled along the water, hand in hand. She was glad the city council had decided to put the pathway in a few years ago. It had been a struggle. Some of the long-standing members of the council didn't like change. But the town had voted for it, and now the pathway meandered along the stream with benches set at intervals and lined with some newly planted pines.

"It's pretty, isn't it?" Annie came up beside her.

"It is. I'm surprised Old Man Dobbs and his anti-everything attitude didn't tank the whole project."

"Walter Dobbs isn't a fan of change. Or a fan of ideas he didn't come up with. When we presented the idea to the city council, we knew it would be a struggle. But I'm glad it happened. I think it's such an improvement for the town." Annie pressed a hot cup of coffee into her hands. "Come on, let's go sit upstairs. It's kind of a mess, but at least the view of the river is spectacular."

They climbed the stairs slowly and settled into two chairs Annie had placed by the new picture window. "When do you think you'll have the upstairs ready to open?"

"I hope within a month or so. I want it open before the May Festival. So many people come to town that weekend. But I still have a lot to do."

"I could send Jason over to help you."

"Your son has enough on his plate at the lodge. I couldn't take him away from that. Besides, I'm pretty handy with all this. I'm glad my father taught me carpentry. I've hired electricians and plumbers, but most of the other work I'm doing myself. Well, I hired workers to put in the fireplace, too."

"The fireplace looks fabulous. I think it will really add to the ambience of the loft." She looked over at the fireplace made with red bricks that had been salvaged from an old building a few towns away.

"I hope so. But there is still so much to do."

"I don't know how you find the time." She knew Annie had been hard at work when the shop was closed on Sundays and Mondays throughout the off-season, but there always seemed to be more to do.

"After I finish the remodel, I'm planning on staying open seven days a week, even during the off-season. At least that's my plan."

"You planning on cloning yourself?" She grinned at Annie.

"I probably should." Annie gave her a rueful smile.

"The slow season is doing a number on our bottom line at the lodge this year. Those really heavy snowfalls on the weekends this winter prevented some of our customers from being able to make it to the lodge. I could use a few more renters to tide us through until it picks up."

"I'll keep an eye out for you. If anyone mentions they need a place, I'll let you know."

"Appreciate that." Nora looked down at the stream rushing along the edge of the pathway. A young woman walked along the path, pushing a stroller with a young child bundled up against the chill. People around here didn't let much keep them inside. She loved that about the town. She turned her attention back to Annie. "So what's on your docket for the rest of the week?"

"I'm going to head over to Mountain Grove College this afternoon. I'm meeting up with a lady who works there about teaching knitting classes here at the shop. I think this upstairs lounge would be the perfect place. We're going to iron out the details."

"Hm, I haven't knit in years. My grandmother taught me when I was a young girl."

Annie grinned. "I remember when you made that knitted tam… it was so lopsided, but you wore it anyway."

"I loved that thing." She shook her head. "I probably still have it tucked away somewhere. I was so proud of it, no matter how silly it looked."

She took one last sip of her coffee. Annie made the best coffee. Even though she bought Annie's special blend of coffee beans for the lodge, it never tasted quite the same. Her friend had some kind of special coffee magic. She set down her mug. "I better go. Jason and I are painting the inside of Serenity Cabin today. Trying to spiff up some of the older cabins before the busy season. Then Beth and the boys are going to stop by for dinner."

"I haven't seen your grandsons in I don't know how long."

"Beth's been busy teaching and the boys are into every sport known to mankind. I haven't even seen much of them recently." Which was why she was looking forward to a family dinner tonight.

"Well, enjoy your dinner."

"I will. You drive safely to Mountain Grove."

"I will."

"Maybe we could catch dinner or lunch later this week."

"Maybe." Annie looked doubtful. "I have so much to do."

ANNIE STOOD by the fountain in the middle of campus. She'd wrapped up her meeting with Nancy, and they'd agreed on days and times for the knitting class at the shop. That was one thing checked off of her long to-do list.

One thing.

So why was she sitting here in the sunshine, perched on the edge of the fountain, instead of hurrying back to the shop? The fresh air beckoned her like a siren call to just sit a spell and linger in the glorious sunshine. She barely had time to breathe these days, much less laze around beside a fountain, no matter how pretty it was. Not that the water was running in it now. But the statues of small children frolicking in the middle of the fountain reminded her of a glimpse of those small moments in life. The ones it seemed people rarely realized were the important moments. She always thought of them as extraordinary, ordinary moments.

She tucked a lock of hair behind her ear with a regretful sigh. Real life beckoned.

She rose and turned away, still deep in thought, and ran smack into the hard chest of a tall man hurrying her direction.

"I'm sorry." She bent down to pick up a paper the man had dropped in the collision, and they bumped heads when he reached for the same pamphlet.

She looked up at him, an apology on the tip of her tongue, and stared directly into his eyes. A raw gasp escaped her lips. She started to tumble backward, but his strong grasp kept her from falling. He hauled her to her feet.

"Annie." His voice was still the same. Warm and deep. Comforting and mesmerizing.

How could his voice enchant her after all this time? That was ridiculous.

She couldn't find her own voice, so instead, she stood and stared at him. Tall and thin with just the tiniest hint of gray threaded through the coffee-brown hair at his temples. His smoky hazel eyes stared back at her. Those eyes that could change from brown to green and back again within a millisecond's time. Those eyes that were staring at her now.

"Nick." She gulped a breath then frowned. "What are you doing here?"

"I, uh... I just took a teaching position here. Temporary. Just until the end of the semester."

"Teaching? I thought..." Her thoughts were muddled, and the world tilted off-kilter. "Last I heard. You know, that last time I saw you... Well, you were going on to medical school."

"I did. I'm just… I'm kind of taking a brief break."

"So you chose Mountain Grove as a place to take that break? After all these years? Why?"

"Because they offered me the position?" He shrugged his broad shoulders. But his look didn't fool her. She knew that look. He was holding something back.

"Why would you come back here? So close to Sweet River Falls? I thought you didn't want anything to do with Colorado." Or her. He hadn't wanted anything to do with her.

"I live in Los Angeles now, and I needed to get away."

Mountain Grove was way too close to Sweet River Falls.

Like twenty minutes too close.

He couldn't just decide to come back here. Not so close to *her* town. Hers. *Not* his. He had the rest of the country to live in. Her pulse thundered in her ears and she swallowed.

He reached out a hand toward her, almost touching her, but not quite. "I couldn't decide if I was going to go over to Sweet River Falls and see you again. But I guess the fates have made that decision for me."

FOR ONCE, Nick thanked the fates. They hadn't been kind to him recently, but now, with this chance meeting with Annie, he hoped his luck would change. His hand hovered just inches away from her arm, but she backed away and he let his hand drop to his side.

His heart still thundered in his chest from their chance meeting. Running into her— literally—after all this time. Fate. It was meant to be.

But the look on her face clearly showed she didn't feel the same way about the fates. Her face held a look of anger and sadness mixed together.

Nick stood in front of her. His Annie. After all these years.

She looked down at the paper in her hand and frowned again. "Rentals?"

He couldn't remember her frowning before. She was always his Annie with the quick smile. The bubbling laugh. The shining blue eyes.

"I need to find a place to stay until the end of the semester. I'm at a motel for now, but looking for somewhere to rent."

A strange look came over her face when he

said that. Her blue eyes clouded, and she frowned. Again. "Well, I'm sure there are plenty of places to rent here in Mountain Grove. You'll find something." She thrust the brochure back at him as if to rid herself of a forbidden book.

"I'm sure I will."

Annie stood in front of him, searching his face, the shocked look still firmly etched on her own. She ran her fingers through the tumble of chin-length blonde hair framing her face. He used to do that. Run his hands through her hair. Her hair had always been so soft. And smelled like flowers after the rain. And enchanted him.

It still did.

"Nick. I've got to go. It was… *nice*… seeing you." She said the words without an ounce of conviction.

"Maybe we could—" He reached out again.

"No, Nick. We couldn't." She spun around and, without a single glance back at him, hurried away down the brick sidewalk.

CHAPTER 3

Nora checked on the large meatloaf she'd put in the oven. It would be done in about thirty minutes. Beth and the boys should be here soon. Nothing like a family dinner to get her puttering around in her kitchen.

The kitchen door opened, and Jason entered the cabin with a burst of cold air. "Mom, I brought that loaf of homemade bread from the lodge like you asked." He set the loaf on the counter and brushed a kiss on her cheek. "Seems like it's been a long time since we had a family dinner."

"It has been." She pointed to the cabinets. "Could you set the table for me?"

"Sure thing." He dropped his coat on a chair, reached into the refrigerator, grabbed a beer, and popped the top. After a long swig, he set it on the counter and gathered a handful of plates and silverware.

The door opened again, and the chaos that was her grandsons swept into the room. "Grams." Trevor and Connor raced to give her a hug.

She wrapped her arms around them. This, this is what life was about. Her family. These boys. She looked over the top of them at her daughter. "You looked tired. Why don't you sit while I finish up dinner?"

"I should help you."

"I'm fine. You rest."

"Hey, you put me to work." Jason grinned as he finished setting the table.

The boys grabbed Jason's hand. "Come on, Uncle Jason. Let's play a game before supper."

"You boys still have homework to do." Beth put an end to the game-playing suggestion.

"How about I help you with your homework?" Jason led them out of the kitchen.

Beth shot him a grateful look and sank onto a chair. "I love those boys dearly, but they clearly want to see if they can exhaust me into a big pile of nothingness."

"Raising kids is hard work." Nora pressed a

tall glass of tea into Beth's hands. "Especially doing it mostly alone."

"It is. But honestly, I think it's almost easier now that Scott is gone. At least the fighting is over. And he wasn't that much help with them anyway." Beth sighed. "Please don't tell me that you never knew what I saw in him, because, honestly, I don't know what I saw in him either."

"We all make mistakes in life. It's what we do after we realize it that counts." Nora put the homemade bread in the oven to warm. "So, how is work?"

"It's going fine. I really have a good class this year. So many of them are eager to learn. A bit crazy with a room of third graders, but I do love that age."

Nora looked doubtfully at Beth. "I'm not sure I could ever handle a room of kids that age. And I *love* kids."

Beth laughed. "It's a challenge some days. Between the class and the boys, I'm surprised I'm still sane. If I am sane…"

"You're doing a great job. I'm proud of you. You've handled the divorce and raising the kids and your job, and you've done it well."

"Thanks, Mom."

"Now, how about we get those kids fed?"

Nora peeked her head out of the kitchen. "Boys, wash up for supper." She smiled at the commotion as they argued about who was going to make it in to get their hands washed first. Everything was a competition between those two.

Boy noise. She so enjoyed an evening of it.

AFTER DINNER, Beth helped her mother with the dishes while Jason helped the boys with their math. It was nice to have a night off from homework duty. Jason was always so patient with them, and they were crazy about their uncle.

"There, that's the last of them." Beth placed the last pan away in the cabinet. "Thanks for having us over. I've had fake dinners the last three nights for the boys. I just can't quite seem to keep up with everything."

"You can ask for help, you know." Her mother eyed her over the top of her glasses.

"I just… I know. But you're really busy, too. You have the lodge to run."

"Well, Jason and I are always here for you if you need anything."

"I know, Mom. Thanks."

Beth walked over to the kitchen doorway. "Boys, five minutes. Then we need to head home."

"I finished my math, but Trevor didn't finish his." Connor stood up and shoved his papers into his backpack.

"He'll be finished in just a few minutes." Jason sat patiently beside Trevor, their two heads bent over her son's worksheet.

As soon as Trevor finished his homework, they headed home. The boys bickered in the back seat. "Come on, boys. Quit arguing."

"Connor says I'm not going to make the baseball team this year."

"Connor, quit teasing your brother."

"Yes, ma'am." Connor said it politely like he'd been taught, but she didn't really believe either of the two boys would ever quit teasing each other. They were one year apart in school and hovered between best of friends and mortal enemies, depending on the day and their moods.

She got them inside and in bed and sank onto the sofa, a small glass of wine in her hand. She still had papers to grade before she could climb into bed herself.

Somehow, when she'd married the high school star quarterback a month after they'd graduated college, she hadn't ever imagined that this is what her life would turn out to be.

Not that she was complaining. She loved the boys. At least she and Scott had gotten that part right. She loved living in Sweet River Falls and loved her teaching job. It was great being so close to her mom and Jason. The boys loved going over to the lodge. Things were mostly perfect, if a bit overwhelming at times.

She set down her glass of wine and grabbed the stack of papers. If she could finish grading these quickly, maybe she'd have time for a nice relaxing bath before bed.

CHAPTER 4

The rentals Nick looked at in Mountain Grove were inadequate, to say the least. One was called an efficiency and had a hot plate and a small dorm-sized fridge. One was listed as a private bedroom but shared a bath with three college kids. A few others were okay, but he found reasons to cross each one off the list. They were not exactly what he was looking for. Not even close.

He circled another place to look at. A lodge in Sweet River Falls. Annie wouldn't be pleased, but he probably wouldn't run into her often.

But was that what he wanted? To *not* run into Annie?

No, he wanted to see her again. Talk to her. Listen to her voice. See her eyes. Those emotions he thought were long gone threatened to pulse through him again.

And he didn't know how he really felt about that.

He glanced down at his new cowboy boots, just beginning to scuff up with one day's wear. He smiled. It did feel right to be back in Colorado. He snatched his cowboy hat off his head and tossed it into the SUV, then headed down the road to Sweet River Falls. The lodge with the rental cabin was on the outskirts of town. Surely that would be okay with Annie, right?

Within twenty minutes he arrived in town. A new, large grocery store sat on the edge of town. He wondered if they'd put Mable's Market out of business. He pulled onto Main Street. The town hadn't changed much. It still had its quaint small-town ambience. New lampposts lined the street, and they'd put planters along the sidewalks. He was pleased to see that all the storefronts were occupied. He'd been secretly afraid that Sweet River Falls would go the way of so many small towns with a dying business district and empty shops. This looked like a bustling, healthy town, and it warmed his heart.

He slowly drove through town and headed

to Sweet River Lodge. From what he could tell, the lodge was nestled between the Sweet River and Lone Elk Lake. Since his teaching schedule was fairly light, he hoped to have lots of time to hike around and be outside in the fresh air. When was the last time he'd taken a hike? It had been years. Probably since he'd left Colorado.

He pulled down the tree-lined road to the lodge and parked near the main office. The fresh scent of pines enveloped him as he swung out of the vehicle. A carved sign hung on a post out front pointing the way to a dining area, the lake, and cabins one through eight. He wondered how many cabins they had here. He looked up at the spectacular view of the mountains in the distance.

Yes, he wanted to rent here. It was perfect. He hoped they still had a cabin available because unless it was a real dump, he was determined to rent it. And maybe even if it was a dump.

Nora looked up from the reception desk as the bell over the front door chimed. A tall man entered and removed his hat.

He looked familiar.

Too familiar.

He crossed the distance in a few quick strides. "I'm looking to—" He stopped mid-sentence when he saw her and searched her face.

"Nora."

"Nick." He couldn't possibly miss her icy tone, could he?

"I… uh… I didn't know you worked here." He twisted the cowboy hat he held clutched in his hands.

"I own the place."

"You do? Oh… I…" He shifted from foot to foot.

"What are you doing here?" She thought she'd never see this man again. The man who'd broken her best friend's heart. And she wasn't sure that Annie had ever gotten over him. He needed to leave. And leave quickly before Annie saw him.

"I was hoping to rent one of your cabins. I saw them listed in the rental brochure."

"I don't think that would be a good idea." She needed the money, but no way was she going to rent to Nick Chambers.

"I really need a place to stay."

"Why are you even in town?" She glared at him.

"I took a teaching job in Mountain Grove."

"Then why aren't you looking to rent over there?"

"They didn't really have what I was looking for."

She'd give him that. Mountain Grove was a college town and catered to large buildings with students packed into them. It would also be hard to find a place to rent mid-semester.

But that wasn't *her* problem.

"How about if you let me rent a cabin just until I can find something else? Please, Nora. I won't cause any trouble."

"What would Annie say if she knew you were back in Colorado?"

"She already does. I ran into her yesterday."

Nora gaped at him in surprise. Annie knew he was in town and hadn't told her? That didn't sound possible.

Though Annie had known she was having the family dinner last night. She was probably waiting to tell her when they met for coffee later today.

The door popped open again with the chime of the bell, and Nora looked up. "Ah…"

This wasn't good.

Annie stood in the sunshine spilling through the open front door.

"Hey, Nora, I thought I'd meet you here instead of—" Annie froze when she saw Nick standing at the reception desk. What was he doing here? In *her* town. Couldn't he just stay in Mountain Grove? Twenty minutes away from her. That's all she asked. Well, she'd prefer twenty hours away, but whatever.

Nick turned at the sound of her voice. "Annie."

"Nick was just leaving." Nora glared at him.

"I was trying to rent a cabin. I didn't have any luck in Mountain Grove. I didn't know Nora owned the lodge."

"I told him to find somewhere else to rent." Nora's eyes flashed with protectiveness.

"I'm sorry. I didn't mean to upset anyone… I just need a place to live for a while." His words sounded reasonable, but they held in their midst a dilemma.

There was no way she was going to let her trouble with Nick cause problems for Nora.

Nora could use every rental dollar she could get during the slow season. A longer term rental would help her out. She crossed over to the desk. "It's okay. Rent him a cabin. I know you have some openings."

Nora looked at her skeptically. "Are you sure?"

"I'm sure."

"Thank you. I appreciate it." Nick smiled at her. That charming smile of his, not that she noticed it.

"Annie, why don't you go on over to my cabin while I check Nick in? I'll be over in a few minutes."

She nodded because standing here with Nick smiling at her was not an option. "Okay." She hurried out the door and back out into the sunshine, trying to keep her pace steady so she didn't look like she was running away.

But she was.

Away from Nick and his smile. Away from the memories threatening to bubble to the surface.

She made herself slow down and walk along the path that wound along the river. The gurgling water did little to calm her nerves. All hopes that yesterday's one chance meeting with

Nick would be her last were dashed into pieces. If he stayed here in Sweet River Falls, she was bound to run into him now and again.

How in the world was she going to deal with that?

She'd just have to keep an eye out and try to avoid him. Hopefully, his job at Mountain Grove college would keep him busy.

Very busy.

She entered Nora's cabin with the not-so-cleverly hidden key under the planter on the front deck. She put on the tea kettle and waited for Nora to join her.

They had a lot to talk about.

"Let's just do a week's rental, what do you say? That should give you enough time to find something suitable over in Mountain Grove." Nora clicked on the keyboard, searching for an empty cabin. Rustic Haven, the one that needed the deck replaced and they hadn't gotten around to painting the inside yet. Furthest cabin from the actual lodge and way away from her own cabin. Though it did have a nice view of the lake and he didn't *deserve* a cabin with a great view. "Cabin fifteen, Rustic Haven."

Nick handed her his credit card. "I really appreciate this, Nora."

"Well, I'd really appreciate it if you'd try to avoid running into Annie. She doesn't need you messing with her life again. I assume you'll be busy in Mountain Grove."

"I actually have a pretty light schedule there."

"That's too bad." Nora knew she was bordering on rude but didn't care. "Try to find something to keep yourself busy and far away from Annie." The last thing Annie needed was Nick to come to town and break her heart again. Just seeing him had to bring up painful memories, and Annie didn't deserve that.

"I'm not here to cause trouble." He took the key she offered him.

"You just *being* here is trouble, Nick." Nora handed him a map of the property. "Take the road out front, make a right. The cabin is by the lake."

"I saw a sign for the dining room."

"Yes, we have a dining room. The hours are on that map. Or you have a small kitchen in your cabin." Not that she wanted him coming to the dining room. She didn't much want to see him any more than Annie did.

"That will be perfect, thanks." He started to walk away from the desk but paused and turned back. "The last thing I want to do is hurt Annie." He walked out the door.

His words sounded sincere, but she didn't believe one word that he said.

"GOODNESS, Annie. Why didn't you tell me Nick was back?" Nora entered the cabin, shrugged off her coat, and dropped it onto a chair.

"I just found out myself. I ran into him in Mountain Grove when I went over there yesterday. I was going to tell you all about it today when I saw you."

"I think Nick being back in town deserved a phone call last night."

Annie sighed. "I just needed some time to process it. I was in shock. I never thought I'd see him again."

Nora grabbed two teacups out of the cabinet. "I'm not sure why he thought taking a job so close to Sweet River Falls would ever be a good idea."

Annie poured the hot water into the teacups. "He said they offered him that teaching position at the college."

"But he went to med school, didn't he? Why's he teaching?"

"I don't know. He said he went to med school, but he was taking a break or something." Annie carried her cup over to the table and sank onto the worn wooden chair. She loved Nora's kitchen with its brightly painted walls and cheerful curtains on a window that looked out over a clearing in the woods. The cabin was nestled into a bit of privacy provided by a small grove of trees, away from the rental cabins, and set right along the Sweet River.

Nora sat down across the table. "Well, it seems like a weird place for Nick to decide to take his break." She dunked her teabag in her cup and swished it around. "I told him to stay far away from you."

Annie smiled. Nora, her best friend since grade school. Always there for her through all of life's ups and downs, as she had been for her friend when Nora's husband had died. They'd seen each other through some rough times, that's for sure. She didn't know what she'd ever do without Nora and didn't ever plan on finding out.

Nora tucked a stray lock of her gray-streaked hair behind her ear. She hadn't changed much in the years they'd been friends. A few wrinkles around her amber eyes, a few gray hairs, but still a warm, welcoming smile.

"Well, I hope Nick does stay away from me. It was a shock to see him again. I just never thought that would happen."

"You should have let me send him packing."

"Nah, it will be okay. I'm sure I won't run into him often." Though, she had run into him twice in two days. That should have used up most of her bad luck, right?

CHAPTER 5

The next morning, Nick stepped out into the crisp air. Just being in Colorado invigorated him. He'd briefly considered going to the dining room at the lodge to eat but decided he didn't want to chance a meeting with Nora. Not that he was afraid of her... but she was an awfully fierce defender of her best friend, and he'd rather not face her this morning.

He'd made up his mind to try and stay away from both Nora and Annie. That's what they both wanted. He could do that.

Only he didn't really *want* to stay away from Annie.

She'd always had a hold on him. A pull. A magnetic force that drew him in that he'd only been able to break free of once. The break that had hurled their lives in separate directions.

He sighed and crossed over to his vehicle. He'd buy groceries on his way home from work and cook at his cabin. That would solve the where to eat problem. But this morning he hadn't even had coffee to brew, and that wasn't cutting it at all.

He climbed into his vehicle and headed into town in search of the much-needed coffee. He could go all the way over to Mountain Grove, but that was way too long to wait for his caffeine fix.

Or he could admit to himself that he wanted to poke around the town he'd grown up in. Walk the streets. See what was new.

Before long he was pulling onto Main Street and parking his car. A few people wandered along the sidewalks. He slid out of the car and his cowboy boots hit the sidewalk. The familiar feeling of wearing the boots comforted him in some strange way. A staple of his life when he was growing up here in Colorado.

A sign with an arrow proclaimed a new riverside walkway. He crossed the street and wandered through a brick courtyard that led to the river. A long pathway wound its way along the river. He looked at it in appreciation, a great addition to the town.

He headed down the pathway until he saw a sign over a door saying Bookish Cafe. Another sign in the window announced 'best coffee in Sweet River Falls,' and that was just what he needed. He pushed in the door and glanced around at the cheerful ambience and welcoming tables. A counter was tucked neatly against the far wall. Just what he was looking for. He headed over to order his coffee.

ANNIE HAD NOWHERE TO HIDE, no time to run. Nick was striding over to the counter. He'd notice her at any moment. She clutched the dishtowel in her hands, frozen to the spot.

Then he saw her. His eyes lit up with surprise, and a warm smile spread across his face. Just as quickly, it disappeared. "Annie, I didn't know you worked here."

She stood there silently, twisting the towel in her hands.

"I... do you want me to go somewhere else for my coffee?" He stood staring at her.

Yes, she wanted him to be getting his coffee

in Los Angeles, or at least Mountain Grove. Heck, he'd rented a cabin. He could brew his own silly coffee. But she wasn't quite brave enough to tell him any of that. She squared her shoulders. "No, of course not. What would you like?"

"A dark roast. Black. Large."

She poured him his coffee and handed it to him. Their fingers briefly brushed, and it took everything in her power not to jerk her hand back and spill the hot liquid all over him. He handed her some money, and she gave him his change, careful to not touch him as she dropped the change into his palm.

"Nice place." He stood in front of her making small talk.

Is that what they'd become? Strangers making small talk? But, strangers, that's what they were now.

"Thanks. It's mine. I mean I own it." She didn't know why she wanted him to know that. Maybe so he'd know she'd moved on after he left and found a good life for herself. Not the one they'd planned together, but a good one nonetheless. She was proud of the shop and all she'd accomplished with her life. A life that hadn't involved going away to some fancy college and on to medical school, leaving everything and everyone behind…

"Wow, Annie, that's impressive. It looks like a great place." He glanced over at the stairway that was roped off. "What's that?"

"I'm expanding upstairs. Putting in a loft room."

"Really? You must be doing really well with the shop."

"I'm working on it in my spare time and on the days the shop is closed."

"I remember all those times your father let us tag along on his construction jobs. He taught us a lot, didn't he? Is he helping you with it?"

Ah, it still caught her off guard when someone asked about her father. She put a steadying hand on the counter. "No… Dad… he passed away."

"I'm so sorry, Annie."

"It was about five years ago." Though it seemed like just yesterday he was popping into the shop for his morning coffee, or stopping by in the afternoon to see if she wanted to go out to eat with him. She missed him every single day. It had just been the two of them for so many years. Ever since her mom had died when Annie had been six years old. From then on it was her father and her against the world. Until… it was just her.

"I know how close you were. It must be really hard."

"It is, but… well, that's life. It was unexpected and happened quickly. I didn't even have time to tell him goodbye. Tell him how much I loved him." She had no idea why she was telling all this to Nick. Except that Nick had been as close to a son as her father ever had.

Well, until Nick had left. Her father had been hurt when Nick had just dropped out of their lives, too. Just thinking about that made her square her shoulders and face Nick.

"Well, I'm sorry I didn't know."

"There's a lot about me that you don't know, Nick." Slightly rude, but honestly, he couldn't come back here and just act like he knew her. He didn't. Not anymore.

"True. It's been a long time."

But he didn't look properly chastised like she'd hoped.

"So you're doing it alone?"

"Most of it. I had someone put in the fireplace and do the electric."

"Can I see it?"

She paused. She could just say it was off

limits due to the construction, but a part of her wanted to show off all she'd done. Show him that she was just fine, thank you very much. She called to one of her workers to cover the coffee bar for her and led the way over to the stairs.

She untied the rope blocking the stairway and climbed the stairs, acutely aware that Nick was one step behind her. The sound of his boots echoed with each step he took.

They entered the loft area, and he let out a low whistle. "Nice job." He walked over to the large picture windows. "The view is fabulous. Sweet River with Sky Haven Mountain in the background. Doesn't get better than this."

His praise warmed her and agitated her at the same time. Why did she even care what Nick thought?

"I really like the pathway the town put in along the river."

"That was a battle, but we finally got it voted in. It's only been finished a few years. Dobbs was firmly against it."

"Old Man Dobbs is still here calling the shots?" Nick shook his head.

"Mostly. He was outvoted on this though. I'm pretty sure he hasn't forgiven Nora or me for campaigning so hard to have it put in."

Nick grinned. "Good for you and Nora. Not many stand up to Dobbs."

She caught herself just before she grinned back at Nick because there was no way she was going to have a friendly conversation with him. No way she was going to encourage him.

No way she could quit staring at his mesmerizing smile...

NICK LOOKED at Annie and knew she was trying her best to stay cool and collected. But he knew her. Knew her so well. She was proud of the pathway along the river, proud of her shop. And she should be.

"I'm glad things have gone well for you since... well, since I left town."

"Since you broke up with me?" Her eyes flashed now, a spitfire of energy and anger.

Ah, he remembered that anger well.

He tilted his head. "Technically, *you* broke up with me."

"Technically, you decided that you wanted to go on to medical school after I waited for you to finish college. And technically you didn't ask me to wait while you went to med school. And *technically*, you didn't object when I said we should end things." She turned to look out the window, hands balled into tight fists, avoiding looking at him. "You were ready to move on. I wasn't going to be the one to hold you back."

"Annie—"

"You were finished with us. With me. You wanted to be free to see what all the world had to offer. You just didn't have the nerve to say the actual words."

She was right. He'd done so much better in college than he'd thought. He'd loved school. When he'd gotten a scholarship to med school, he couldn't resist it. He'd been surprised and honored. He couldn't turn down a chance like that. And he'd wanted to be able to go anywhere, do anything after med school. And Annie had always wanted to live in Sweet River Falls.

"You were braver than I was, Annie. Brave enough to say the words. I *am* sorry I hurt you. I am. I know we'd made plans. Plans for a life together."

"Plans change."

He couldn't mistake the pain in her words. "They do. Life throws us unexpected curves. I know you were ready to settle down... and I just wasn't. I wanted to see all that life out there had to offer." And how had that worked out for him? He scrubbed a hand over his face, blocking out the memories of his life in Los Angeles. Blocking out the reason he'd taken this job in Colorado.

"Did you find everything you were looking for?" Her voice was so low he could barely hear her.

"I… did. Sort of."

"Well, then everything worked out for both of us, didn't it? The way it was meant to be." She turned to him and pasted on a cheerful face, but he could still see the pain in her eyes.

"I guess so."

He turned away from the window and looked around the loft area. "You still have quite a bit of work left to do, don't you?"

And undoubtedly she missed having her father work with her, by her side. Annie had always loved her father and adored working with him when she could.

Annie looked grateful he'd changed the subject from them to the loft. "I do. Lots. I was hoping to open for the May Festival, but I just don't think I'll make it. The town is so full of tourists that weekend, I could use the extra space, and it would be a good time for the grand opening. But I'm trying not to hire extra help for anything I can do myself. Can't really afford to."

"I could help you." He was surprised when the words just spilled from his lips. "I'm finding myself with more free time than I expected. I'm used to staying busy. I *want* to stay busy." Really busy. So busy that he didn't have time to sit and think. "I did construction work on the side when I was in med school to help pay my bills. All that carpentry your father taught us came in handy. Let me help you."

"I couldn't let you do that."

"Of course you could."

"I don't think that's a very good idea..."

"You want to finish it before the May Festival, don't you?" He took another tact. "We were friends once, good friends. Let's just call this a friend helping a friend."

He could tell the exact moment she wavered. And frowned. He was already tired of seeing her frown. He wanted to put smiles back on her face. He missed those smiles.

"I do want it finished before the festival. I guess you could help..." She sounded like she was trying to convince herself.

"Great, that's settled." He rushed the words before she had a chance to change her mind. "How about I come by after work today and we can go over your plans and you can tell me what I can do to help?"

"Are you sure?" He could clearly see the doubt in her eyes.

"I'm sure. I'll be here about six."

CHAPTER 6

Beth tugged open the door to Brooks Gallery and waved to the worker waiting on a customer. She headed to the backroom. Her friend Sophie was singing quietly as she bent over a bench, hard at work on creating one of her silver jewelry pieces. "Hey, Soph."

"Beth, is it five already?" Sophie glanced at her watch.

Beth laughed. "You always get lost in your work."

"I do sometimes." Sophie held up a silver bracelet with blue stones. "What do you think?"

"I think it's lovely. What are those stones? They're so pretty."

"Denim lapis."

"Wonderful as always."

Sophie stood and stretched. "Are the boys with your mom?"

"Yes, they're spending the night with her tonight. They cooked it up when we were over there for dinner last night. We've been so busy that they haven't spent much time with her lately. They had big plans for popcorn and a movie marathon."

"So you have the whole evening to yourself?"

"I do. Let's make the best of it."

"Let me tell Melissa that we're headed upstairs."

Sophie came back a minute later. "Melissa's going to lock up." She led the way up the back stairs and opened the door to her apartment above the gallery. The entire upper floor was a rustic, open concept room. The kitchen in one corner and a sitting area in front of a big picture window overlooking the tumbling water of Sweet River. A partitioned off area designated the bedroom.

Sophie crossed over to the refrigerator and pulled out a bottle of white wine. Beth grabbed two glasses. They walked over to the two comfortable chairs in front of the picture window and settled in as they had so many times before. Their favorite spot for happy hour.

Sophie cocked her head to one side, then the other. "I really should take more breaks when I'm working." She reached up to rub her shoulder.

"Remember when we had big plans to go to the gym five times a week?" Beth shook her head. "I barely have time to breathe, much less exercise."

"We do have our once a week evening yoga class."

"The only reason I make it there most of the time is because I know you'll be there."

"Guilt is a powerful motivator." Sophie grinned. "I'm not really any good at yoga, but I sure enjoy it."

"We used to go hiking on the weekends, too."

"Well, I took over the gallery, and you had two kids, got divorced, and have a teaching job. Things have changed since high school."

Beth looked down at the rushing water in the stream. "Things have changed. Look at how well everything is going with the gallery now. Your parents would have been so proud."

"I hope so." Sophie gazed off into the distance.

Beth reached over and squeezed her friend's hand. "They would be proud. I know you miss them. I miss them too. They were great people."

"They were." Sophie tucked a wayward lock of blonde hair behind her ear.

Sophie's parents had died in a car accident five years ago. Sophie had given up her job teaching music at the high school and taken over running the gallery her parents had owned. Beth wondered if running the gallery was what Sophie really wanted to do with her life, but she insisted it was. There was no way she'd let her parents' dream die.

"Anyway..." Sophie turned and smiled. "What's new in your life?"

"Nothing. Same old, same old. Working. Chasing boys." Beth took a sip of her wine.

Sophie laughed. "Chasing boys sure doesn't mean what it used to mean to us, does it?"

"How times have changed." Beth smiled. "Oh, but here's something new. Mom said Annie's old boyfriend is back in town."

"Annie's been single as long as I've known her. I can't even picture her with a boyfriend."

Sophie's forehead creased. "How long ago did she date him?"

"Like back when Mom and Annie were in high school. I guess there was some kind of messy breakup when he finished college. Annie was crushed. I wonder if that's why she rarely dates. Well, at least I've rarely heard Mom talk about Annie dating anyone."

"Must be strange to have him back here after all that time."

"Well, it gets stranger. Mom rented one of the cabins to him. He's teaching in Mountain Grove through the end of the semester."

"Your mom rented a cabin to someone who broke Annie's heart?"

"She said Annie insisted. But knowing Annie, she insisted because she knows that Mom and Jason can use all the income they can get right now. It's been a hard winter for the lodge."

"It's been hard at the gallery, too. So many harsh days and weekends when we'd normally have tourists in town."

"Well, hopefully, you all will have a fabulous tourist season this summer."

"I bet your boys are looking forward to the summer."

"They are. They love when I work at Sweet

River Lodge during the summers when school is out. They love hanging around the lodge. Jason usually has them helping out around the lodge, too. Not to mention he takes them hiking and fishing."

"He's great with the boys."

"He's a great brother, but don't ever let him know I said that." Beth grinned. She took another sip of her wine and glanced at her watch. "You about ready to head over to Bookish Cafe and grab a salad?"

"Ready when you are." Sophie stood up.

They put their glasses in the sink, grabbed their jackets, and headed down Main Street for dinner.

WHAT HAD SHE BEEN THINKING? Was she out of her mind? Why in the world had she accepted Nick's offer of help? Annie swiped at an imaginary streak on the window. She glanced at her watch for like the hundredth time in the last twenty minutes.

If she'd had Nick's cell phone number, she would have called and cancelled. No, better yet, *texted* and cancelled. Made up some excuse why he couldn't come this evening. She straightened a stack of books and adjusted some pamphlets near the door. Her customers were scattered around the shop, browsing books or eating sandwiches or salads at the tables in the cafe area. She wandered over and straightened some chairs at the empty tables.

And glanced at her watch yet again.

The door open and she swirled around.

Not Nick. Relief rushed through her, promptly replaced with uneasiness because he was bound to show up any minute.

"Annie, hi." Beth crossed over and gave her a big hug. "How've you been? I haven't seen you in forever."

Annie hugged Beth and smiled at Sophie. "I hear you've been busy."

"I have been, but Sophie and I are having a girl's night out. Mom's got the boys tonight. We came in for some salads."

The door opened again, and Annie froze.

"You okay?" Beth reached out and placed a hand on Annie's arm. "Annie?"

"What? Yes. I'm fine."

Nick crossed the distance in a few strides and flashed his treacherous smile. Everyone in the shop faded away for a brief moment while she let his smile settle all around her. Then she quickly stepped back as if sliding out of the circle of influence his smile had over her.

"I'm reporting for duty." He still smiled, but she was safely out of its reach. Kind of.

"Nick, ah…"

Beth and Sophie stood watching her.

"Um, Nick. This is Beth, and this is Sophie. Beth is Nora's daughter."

"Nice to meet you." Nick stared at Beth. "You're the spitting image of your mother."

Beth laughed. "I hear that all the time. So you know my mom?"

"I knew her a long time ago. I'm staying at Sweet River Lodge now."

"Oh…" A look of putting two-and-two together crossed Beth's face.

"Nick is an old… friend." Annie didn't know how else to describe him. She could just say that Nick was the man who crushed her heart and her dreams ever so many years ago.

Nick seemed oblivious to her introduction turmoil. "More emphasis on the *friend* than the old." Nick winked.

Beth grabbed Sophie's arm. "We'll just go grab our salads and let you two… do whatever it is you're planning on doing."

Annie watched as they walked away, their heads bent together, obviously talking about her and Nick. Nora must have told Beth about him.

Now it was just her and Nick.

She should tell him it was a bad idea for him to help her.

She'd changed her mind.

He should leave.

CHAPTER 7

Nick spun around at the sound of a crash from the corner. The wails of a young boy filled the shop. He froze in place, a terrible fear immobilizing him, torn between rushing to help, like he'd been trained, or running out the door. He fought back the now familiar panic and forced himself to follow Annie who was already rushing over to the table in the corner.

"Jimmy, are you okay?" Annie knelt beside the boy and his mother.

Nick joined her and bent down to one knee. "Hey there, son. Let me take a look."

The boy looked up at him through tear-filled eyes.

Nick quickly assessed the situation as so

many years had taught him to do. "Annie, do you have a first aid kit?"

"I do." Annie jumped up and hurried away. She was back quickly with the kit in her hand.

"I'm Dr. Nick, by the way."

"I'm Jimmy." The boy sniffled.

"Jimmy, you've got a bit of an ouch on your forehead. I'm going to check it out for you, okay?"

He could do this. It was a simple cut. Not a life and death decision. Nothing he did here would hurt the boy. It was simple first aid. He glanced at his hand, surprised to see it shaking. He willed his hands to steady, opened the first aid kit, and slipped on a pair of gloves from the kit. Soon his training and muscle memory kicked in as he deftly cleaned the gash, put on some butterfly bandages, then placed another bandage over that.

The boy looked up at him with wide, trusting, bright blue eyes. The blue eyes almost did him in, but he consciously told himself to ignore them. "There, you're all set. You'll have quite the story to tell your friends at school tomorrow."

The boy swiped at his cheek, wiping away

the last of his tears. "Thanks, Dr. Nick. That didn't even hurt much."

"You were very brave." Nick turned to the boy's mother hovering over them. "I think he'll be okay. But of course, if you have any concerns, you should contact his doctor. If he gets a headache, nausea, or dizziness, get him checked out. Never can be too careful when you conk your head."

"Thank you so much for your help." The mom turned to the boy and wrapped him in a tight hug.

"Mom, you're squeezing me to death." The boy squirmed.

"I'm just glad you're okay. But what have I told you about leaning back in your chair?"

"I know, I know." His long-suffering tone belied his tender age. "Maybe I'll remember not to now."

Nick got to his feet. "Your mom has good advice. Chairs can be tricky things."

The boy reached up and gingerly touched the bandage on his forehead. "Yeah, they sure can."

"I'm so sorry, Sheila." Annie reached out and took the mom's hand.

"It's not your fault, Annie. Jimmy knows better."

"Well, I'm sorry he got hurt." She turned to Jimmy. "If it's okay with your mom, I bet we could get you a scoop of ice cream."

"Can I, Mom?"

The woman nodded and sank into her chair. Nick could see relief was flooding through her, that moment when the adrenaline rush ebbs and all a person wants to do is sit and realize it's all over.

Annie walked away, but stopped and turned to look back at him. "I'll meet you upstairs?"

He nodded, then turned to Jimmy's mom. "He'll be fine."

"Thank you." She looked up at him with grateful eyes.

He headed up the stairs, needing a moment to compose himself. At least he hadn't frozen. Well, not for long anyway. He was glad he'd been able to help the boy. He crossed over to the large picture window and stood in the semi-darkness. He looked down at his hands. They were shaking again. He balled them into fists and stared out at the river.

Annie said goodbye to Jimmy and his mother and slowly climbed the stairs to the loft area. Nick had been great with Jimmy, comforting and proficient at the same time. She'd seen a softer side of Nick, one she wasn't expecting. In her mind, he was always the callous man who had left her without a thought about her feelings.

Though, maybe she'd made up that version of him to help protect herself. They'd both been young and wanted different things back then. She knew that. But when he'd left, he'd taken a huge chunk of her heart and her soul with him.

She reached the top of the stairs and saw Nick standing by the window looking out into the darkness. She crossed over to stand beside him. He looked down at her and smiled. "Jimmy all set with his ice cream?"

"Yes, he and Sheila left with Jimmy licking his ice cream cone on the way out."

The moonlight filtered in the window, illuminating the planes of his face, casting a silvery light into the room. She looked sideways at him, glancing at his profile when he turned to look back out the window. The profile that was so much the same, and yet different. She brought her thoughts back to the present. "You were good with Jimmy. Did you work with kids?"

Goodness, maybe he had a child of his own.

But she couldn't quite make herself ask him that. "I realize I don't even know what kind of medicine you do. Or did."

"I do... *did*... pediatrics." He took a deep breath and reached up to rake his hand through his hair. "Pediatric oncology."

She noticed his hands were a bit unsteady and frowned. "You okay?"

"What? Sure." He crammed his hands into his pockets.

"So you worked with kids with cancer? Wow, that's a tough job." She couldn't imagine that. But it took a caring person to choose that field, to try and make a difference for the kids. "That must be really hard."

"It is." His voice was low, but she didn't miss the edge of pain hidden in his words.

That tortured tone made her want to reach out and touch him, but of course, she didn't. Couldn't. "Is that why you needed to take a break? Just to get away from it for a while?"

"Something like that."

She waited for him to explain more but soon realized that was all he was going to give her. She couldn't quite get over this different side of Nick. So different than the Nick she'd painted a picture of all these years. The self-centered, what's-in-it-for-him Nick. The one who could just carelessly walk away from her after years of planning a life together.

He turned to look at her, closing the book on discussing his life. "So, do you have drawings for the loft area? Let's look at them. Make a plan of attack and see if we can get this loft of yours finished by the May Festival."

And just like that, the moment was over.

She crossed the room, flipped on the overhead lights, and led the way to a table in the corner where she'd spread out the drawings for the addition. She smoothed out the wrinkled pages, worn from countless times of poring over all the little details.

"Over there is where I still need to frame in a wall and drywall it." She pointed. "I'm going to leave the bricks exposed on that wall over there."

"It's going to look nice, Annie. You did a good job maximizing the space here and keeping an open feeling with that great view."

His praise warmed her even though she

didn't want it to. She didn't really want anything from him.

Well, except she *would* accept his help with the loft. He owed her that much, didn't he?

Nick sat in front of the fire in his cabin late that night after coming back from Annie's. He nursed a bottle of beer, but mostly just stared into the flames. His stockinged feet were propped up on the hearth and he'd left the lights out. The room was faintly illuminated by the dancing flames casting flickering shadows on the walls of the cabin.

He sat wrapped in the cozy light and the warmth of the fire. It had been forever since he'd just sat. Not doing charts. Not reading medical journals. Not reading research papers on some new technique that had come out to try and battle the unending stream of types of cancer these kids had to fight. Not thinking of death and pain.

He just sat.

Like a normal person.

He took another sip of the beer. He'd almost lost it when Jimmy had fallen, but he'd managed to pull himself together. What kind of doctor panics when a kid is hurt and needs him?

The kind of doctor he'd finally become. One who didn't know who he was anymore or what he was going to do.

A doctor hiding out from his real life.

If only relaxing in front of the fire like this and working beside Annie could be real life. But it wasn't. He'd been trained for years in his field. He had a lot he could do, could give.

He just wasn't sure there was anything left of him to do that giving anymore.

CHAPTER 8

"Are you crazy? He's helping you with the loft?" Nora looked at Annie and scowled. "I'm not thinking that's very smart."

"It probably isn't." Annie took a sip of her coffee while she perched on the edge of her desk. "But, honestly, I can use the help if I want to get the loft area open by the May Festival."

Nora looked closely at her friend. She couldn't tell what was going on in Annie's mind. Well, that wasn't exactly the truth. Annie was confused. Nick always used to be able to charm her.

Evidently, he still could.

"So he came here last night?" Nora settled into a chair in Annie's office.

"He did. And while he was here, Jimmy Nelson fell and split his head open. Nick cleaned him all up and bandaged him. He was really great with Jimmy. Gentle."

Nora knew that look. Annie was softening towards Nick. "Annie, you need to be careful."

"I know." Annie sighed. "I just… well, I saw a different side of him last night."

"A different side than the man who crushed your heart? Crushed it so badly that you've never let yourself really be interested in anyone since then?"

"It's not that I've never been interested in anyone. Not exactly."

"Right, there was poor Leonard. You guys dated for like ten years. Nothing ever came of it."

"Leonard was a nice… well, friend. Nothing more."

"So tell me another name of someone who you've gone out with more than a handful of times."

"I don't know. I'm sure there have been some."

Nora cocked her head. "Really?"

"Well, maybe not. Not really. But I'm fine. I like my life the way it is. I love it actually."

"I know you do. So maybe playing with fire... or Nick... however you want to look at it, isn't so smart."

"I know." Annie looked down at her hands.

"But he's leaving soon and going back to his real job, right?" Why couldn't Annie see what a big mistake this was? Well, she knew the answer to that. Because... *Nick*.

"He is. I found out he's a pediatric oncologist."

Nora let out a low whistle. "Wow. That's some job."

"I know, right? No wonder he's taking a break and teaching this semester. I would think a job like that would just eat on you."

"I just can't reconcile my vision of Nick, selfishly leaving you and taking off, with Nick the pediatric oncologist." Nora stretched out her legs and noticed her boots could use a good cleaning. Or at least knock some of the dirt off from the ever-present mud left from the thawing snow. She hoped she hadn't tracked much into Annie's shop. Though everyone was used to muddy footprints this time of year. It just came with living here.

She looked up at Annie, who was staring

into her coffee cup, possibly avoiding her and her questions.

Annie finally looked up from her perusal of her cup. "He's coming over Sunday afternoon while the shop is closed. We're going to see if we can get that last wall up."

"I could still send Jason over. He could help." And maybe intervene in between Annie and Nick. Nora wasn't sure she wanted them to spend any more time alone.

Her friend had one fatal flaw, one weakness. And that weakness was Nick Chambers.

Annie shook her head. "No, I think Nick and I can get it. Besides, I know Jason is busy at the lodge. You have to get everything ready for the May Festival too, and your busy season. Don't worry about me. I promise I'll be careful. I'm grateful for Nick's help with the remodel, but that's all it is."

But somehow she didn't believe Annie's words, even if Annie did. She could see the look in her friend's eyes. The look that said Nick was sliding back into her life—and maybe into her heart—if he'd ever even been gone from it.

PROMPTLY AT NOON ON SUNDAY, Nick showed up at the back door to Bookish Cafe. Annie let him in like it was the most natural thing in the world. Let Nick into the shop. Let Nick into her life...

He smiled at her as he entered. She ignored his smile. Mostly.

She led them up to the loft and over to the table with her plans.

"Okay, let's tackle this wall." Nick pulled on work gloves, and they started to work without any mindless chatter.

Which suited Annie just fine, thank-you-very-much.

Only soon she wanted him to talk to her about something other than measurements of boards and hand-me-the-hammer. Wanted to know more about his life since he'd left Sweet River Falls. Wanted to know why he needed a break from his work.

Wanted to know why she hadn't been enough to keep him here all those years ago...

That thought was always on her mind these days. Oh, she knew they'd wanted different things, and her older self realized she'd been unwilling to give up Sweet River Falls for him, either. Sometimes love didn't win, didn't conquer all.

She resolutely pushed all thoughts of the past from her mind. They worked quietly side by side, with few words, until they finished the framework for the new wall. She'd forgotten how well they worked together. So many hours of helping her father at his job sites when Nick would come home from college for the summer break and needed to earn money for school.

They finally sat by the window to take a break. Annie got them both a cold soda, and she perched on a chair, sipping the drink. "Thanks for your help, Nick. That would have taken me forever to do it myself."

"Much easier with two people." He stretched out his long, jean-clad legs.

His boots looked fairly new, with just a few scuffs on them. She was pretty certain he'd bought them since his arrival in Colorado. Along with his newish-looking jeans and the blue flannel shirt he had on today. But she figured he hadn't had much use for that type of clothing in Los Angeles.

"You're staring at me," Nick said matter-of-factly.

The heat of a blush rushed across her cheeks. "No, I… well, I guess I was. Looking at your new mountain clothes."

He grinned. "Yep, a bit different than my California wardrobe." He rubbed his hand on his leg. "I've missed the feel of jeans. Though these could use about a dozen washings to soften them up."

"So the boots are new, too?"

He smiled. "They are. Remember my old boots? I loved those things. I don't know whatever happened to them. Must have gotten rid of them in one of my moves."

She knew darn well what happened to them. Should she confess now? She looked out the window, then back at Nick. "I... well, you left them here when you... went away. Remember, you were staying with Johnny when you came to town that weekend. You were in such a hurry to leave that you left some of your things. Johnny gave them to me to send to you. But I never did."

"Can't say I blame you."

"I... well, I burned them."

"You what?" His eyes widened.

"Burned them. You have any idea how long it takes to burn the soles of cowboy boots?"

Nick laughed. "No, I guess I don't."

She grinned at him. "It was kind of cathartic to toss them into the fire. Though, I did have to finally just bury the remains of the soles."

"Well, that solves the mystery of the missing boots."

"So it looks like you'll just have to keep breaking in those new ones."

"Guess I will…" He winked at her. "But I'm not planning on leaving these behind when I leave. Don't want another perfectly good pair of boots burned up."

There it was. When he leaves. He would be leaving. She had to remind herself. This was just a momentary thing.

She sat up straight. "Well, I guess we should wrap it up. It's been a long afternoon. I do appreciate your help."

"No problem." Nick got to his feet and reached out a hand for her.

She couldn't just not take his offered hand, could she? She slowly placed her hand in his. A shot of heat rushed up her arm. She quickly jumped up and grabbed her hand back. Away from his firm grip. Away from the connection.

"So, how about a small payment for my help?" He cocked his head to one side and smiled. That darn smile of his.

Annie frowned. He knew she didn't have

extra money to hire someone to help her. She'd explained all that. She'd thought he was just offering to help because they were friends. Because… why *was* he helping her?

"Do you still make the best fried chicken in town?" He winked at her. "I could use a home-cooked meal."

"I…" Did she want to have him over to her house? No, of course not. But how could she refuse? He'd helped her all afternoon. "Yes, I still fry chicken. Not sure it's the best in town though."

"Bet it still is." Nick flashed that smile at her.

Again with the smile. Could he ever talk without smiling? "Okay, okay. Fried chicken it is. Tomorrow night?"

"I'll be there." Nick nodded with a self-satisfied grin on his face.

What had she done? Working side by side was one thing. But sitting at a table with him, talking, nothing keeping them too busy to discuss things? That was just seriously *crazy*.

Nick reached for his jacket. "Oh, hey. I don't know where you live now."

"I live in my father's house. Well, my house now, I guess."

"Okay. I'll see you about six?"

She nodded and watched him head down the stairs. What madness had she gotten herself into?

Man, if Nora found out... her friend would kill her.

CHAPTER 9

Nick hurried back to his cabin after teaching on Monday and got ready to head to Annie's. He put on a clean shirt. He'd picked up flowers and a bottle of wine on his way home. He wanted the evening to be relaxing and...

And what? Where was all of this heading?

He couldn't believe he'd asked himself over to dinner. But the words had just slipped out. Words had a way of doing that around Annie.

He grabbed his jacket and headed out the door. Nora came out of the cabin next to his carrying a laundry basket. "Nick, you headed out for dinner?"

"Yep. Having dinner with Annie. She's making me her fried chicken."

Nora scowled. "I thought you were going to stay away from her."

"I… well, I'm helping her with the remodel."

"So I heard. Do you think that's a good idea?"

"She needs the help." He shrugged. Nora was just being protective of Annie, he got that. But he had no plans to complicate Annie's life. He was *helping* her. That's all this was. And maybe getting a good home-cooked meal in the process.

"Just be careful, Nick. I don't want to see Annie hurt again."

He stood staring at Nora. He had no plans to hurt Annie. He hadn't planned on hurting her all those years ago either. He let out a long sigh. "We're just friends now."

Nora didn't look convinced.

Is that what they were? Friends? Maybe less, maybe more? He nodded at Nora and climbed into the SUV. He pulled out onto the main road and followed the familiar turns to Annie's house. The one she'd grown up in. The one he'd spent so many hours at. He realized he was eager to see it again.

Or maybe he was eager to see Annie again.

Things were getting complicated. If he wasn't careful, he was going to overanalyze everything just like Annie did. He smiled at the thought.

He pulled up in front of her house, slightly surprised it looked just the same, but glad it did. He climbed the front steps to the long, wooden deck. A porch swing still hung at the far end with a couple of rocking chairs in front of the big picture window. The cabin was nestled in a grove on Ponderosa Creek, a small stream that branched off of the Sweet River. Annie's father —well, Annie now—owned ten acres of this paradise. Enough for privacy, but close enough to hop into town.

The scent of evergreen cascaded around him. The wind picked up, and he'd heard there was a chance of a spring snow later this week. He wouldn't mind being here in Sweet River for another snowfall. He hadn't seen snow in years, except for some fake snow at a Christmas party he'd been invited to last year in L.A.

He juggled the wine bottle, knocked on the door, and waited patiently for Annie to answer. Maybe not so patiently. He shifted from foot to foot, holding the flowers in one hand and grasping the bottle of wine in the other.

The door swung open and light spilled out onto the deck. She stood in faded jeans, stockinged feet, and a yellow sweater.

She looked...

He couldn't even think of the word.

Wonderful. Lovely. Beautiful.

He thrust the flowers toward her, speechless.

"You didn't have to do that." Annie took the flowers, realizing her response was not exactly gracious. "Come in."

He entered the cabin like he had a million times when he'd come to see her when they were younger. Much younger. He paused just inside the door and slowly looked all around the main room of the cabin. "It looks so much the same."

"Yes, I know." Why did that sound like an apology?

"No, I like that it's the same. Always loved your father's cabin. Your cabin now."

Annie closed the door behind him. "I haven't really changed anything. I did take down all the posters from the wall of my bedroom." She grinned. "Painted the walls a pale yellow.

Oh, and bought a new bedspread." Now, why had she told him that?

"You didn't take over the master bedroom?"

"I… no, I still feel like that's Dad's room." She shrugged. "Besides, I just feel more comfortable in my old room."

Nick slipped off his jacket and hung it on the coat rack by the door. "I brought us some wine." He held out the bottle. "A dry red. I didn't know what you liked now, so I just guessed. Figured this was better than the terrible cheap beer we used to drink."

"I'm sure it will be lovely." Annie turned. "Come on back to the kitchen." She heard his steps echoing on the wood floors as he followed her. It was so strange to have Nick back here at the cabin.

"Well, this is new." Nick stood in the middle of the kitchen.

"I did have to replace some appliances. The fridge died. I replaced that beat up white one with this stainless one. Then replaced the stove, too. Couldn't get the old one to stay lit, and the oven wasn't heating evenly. They both were a million years old, anyway."

"Still no dishwasher?"

"No, I prefer to just wash dishes by hand.

It's not like there's ever a crowd here." She crossed to a cabinet and got out an old mason jar, filled it with water, and placed the flowers in it. "The flowers look nice, don't they?"

"Lots of yellow flowers in that bouquet. You still like yellow, don't you?"

"Of course." She glanced down at her sweater. "I feel like half my wardrobe is some shade of yellow."

"I remember well. Glad to see it hasn't changed." His eyes sparkled with laughter, and he held up the wine bottle. "Hey, you got a wine opener? I could open the wine for us."

She handed him the opener and peeked into the oven at the loaf of bread just beginning to brown.

Nick poured them both a glass of wine and handed one to her. He leaned against the counter as she put the first pieces of chicken into the frying pan.

It was all so familiar. Nick lounging in the kitchen as she cooked. She'd always done the cooking for her father while she lived with him. She'd finally moved out into an apartment of her own in her thirties, but her father hadn't really been a fan of the change. But she'd thought it was the right thing to do. She should live on her own. It was expected at some time in her life. But she had still come over and cooked for both of them a couple times a week.

She'd lived in that same apartment until her father passed away, and then she'd moved back here. She could sometimes still feel him here with her. She liked touching things he used to touch. Running her hand along the furniture pieces he'd built for the cabin, still feeling like she was connected with him.

"You okay? You look lost in thought."

"What? Yes, I'm fine." Just seeing Nick here at the cabin brought up visions of the past. Somewhat comforting and somewhat unsettling.

Nick shifted his stance against the counter. "The chicken smells great. And is that your homemade bread I smell baking?"

"It is. Haven't baked a loaf in a long time. We'll have to see how it turns out."

She finished up dinner while Nick set the table, and they both slipped into their chairs across from each other. She panicked for a moment when an overwhelming urge to run swept over her. Which was ridiculous. She was just having dinner with Nick. It wasn't anything more.

So why the panic?

She steadied her nerves and brought up the weather. That was safe. They talked weather and the forecast for the upcoming snow storm. They discussed Nick's teaching job while he devoured every piece of chicken, two helpings of green beans, and a sizable chunk of the homemade bread.

He leaned back in his chair after the meal, sipping on his wine. "That was remarkable. Better than I remembered. I can't tell you the last time I've had a home cooked meal."

"Don't you cook for yourself?"

"Nope. Rarely have time. Occasionally I might grill out a steak, but that's about it. I mostly grab food at the hospital or the diner across from it."

"I thought doctors were supposed to be health nuts and eat nutritious meals."

"Maybe. I mostly just forge my way through the day."

"That can't be good." She frowned. "You should make it a point to eat better."

"I probably should."

NICK WAS SURPRISED to find he liked Annie fussing over his eating habits. It was a strange feeling to have someone care what he did or what he ate. Annie was looking down at her plate now like she'd crossed some line with her comment. But that frown of hers? That had to go.

"You sure frown a lot now."

Annie looked up in surprise. "I do?"

"You do. You used to smile all the time."

"I… I don't even know what to say to that." Her forehead began to crease into a frown, but she caught herself.

"I didn't mean that as a criticism, just an observation." He'd probably put his foot in it now. It had been forever since he'd had a conversation with a woman about anything other than medicine. He rarely dated.

But then, this wasn't a *date*.

He quickly changed the subject… but not back to food because he wasn't sure he wanted more talk about his lousy eating habits. He vowed to change them. Well, at least he'd try. "So, how long have you owned Bookish Cafe?"

"A long time. I worked at Bet's Books for a while—do you remember that shop? I also helped out my dad with his business. I ended up keeping the accounts for his construction company. When Bet decided to retire, I bought her shop. Then when this space that I'm in now came available, I moved the shop. I expanded some and added the cafe. Then I added on the gift section and souvenir area. A little bit of everything. It's still mostly the bookstore, though. The other things just help to pay the bills."

"You've sure done a lot with it. You always did have a good head for business."

A blush crossed her face, and she reached for her napkin, carefully folded it, and placed it beside her plate. "With people reading ebooks now, and online magazines, it's been a slow decline in book sales. I do think people still like to come and browse and hang out. I try to make it a fun place to come and visit with friends. Some of the people outside of town who can't get internet service come and grab the Wi-Fi, too."

"I'm impressed, Annie."

He watched while the lovely blush deepened across her cheeks.

"So, tell me more about your work. I mean your work in Los Angeles." She changed the subject, and just like that his heart started to pound.

He didn't like to talk about his work in L.A. At least not anymore. So he deftly avoided her question. "I've actually applied for a research job. It's in Houston. They're doing some cutting-edge research, and I'd like to be a part of it." And it wouldn't involve day in and day out care of patients. It would be safe.

"That sounds interesting."

"Anyway, that's my plan. If I get the job. We'll see. It takes them forever to make a decision. Lots of bureaucracy. But in the meantime, I have my teaching job." *Yes, let's talk about my safe teaching job.* It was a simple job. He could impart his knowledge to these young, hopeful students. These almost-doctors who hadn't had time to become jaded.

"So your plan is to give up your practice and go totally into research? Won't you miss the kids?"

"I…" He couldn't begin to answer that. He did miss the kids. Especially the few that managed to capture his heart, even though he knew he shouldn't let that happen. But sometimes, he couldn't help it. Sometimes a child or two just sneaked in and took hold. But with a research job, he wouldn't have to worry about that.

Annie was still looking at him, waiting for an answer.

"I think I can help more kids with research than one on one." He'd leave it at that. A simple statement. No more hugs from kids he'd managed to get into remission. No more grateful tears from their parents.

But also, no more telling a parent that there was no hope left for their child, nothing else he could do for them except try and keep them comfortable. And even then, sometimes he failed at that.

He scrubbed a hand over his face. "Anyway, let me help you with the dishes." He stood up, grabbed his plate, and headed over to the sink, ending all talk of his prior career and the choices he'd made.

CHAPTER 10

The next day after teaching, Nick was convinced he'd probably die without a good cup of coffee to get him through the afternoon. He'd just stop by Bookish Cafe and grab that best cup of coffee in Sweet River Falls.

He entered the store and looked around. Customers sat in groups at the tables, chatting, eating, or sipping coffee. A few browsed through the racks of books. A young couple sat at a table in the corner, their heads bent together, looking at a laptop screen. He searched the store and saw Annie reading to a group of children in the corner. The children sat in rapt attention on mats on the floor as she held up a book to show them the pictures as she read along.

He wondered if there was anything she

didn't do to keep this store up and running, to make it a regular meeting place for the townsfolk and tourists in town. He crossed to the counter and ordered a large black coffee, paid for an outdoor life magazine, then settled down at a table in the back to enjoy the fragrant brew.

Okay, really he was waiting for Annie to finish.

He'd had a good time at her home last night, except for all the talk about his career. The rest was nice, though. A simple evening. Good company. Great food. It just seemed so... normal. Was that really how most people lived? Not stressing over life and death decisions?

He paged through the magazine, browsing through ads for hiking gear. He wouldn't mind getting in some hiking time while he was here. Though he'd have to buy gear for that, too. Hiking boots, backpack, and water bottle at the very least. He grabbed his phone and started typing in a list of supplies to get at Alpine Outfitters.

"Hey, Nick."

He looked up to find Annie standing beside his table. "Hi, I came in for your famous coffee."

"You planning on hiking?" She nodded at the magazine open to an ad for hiking gear.

"I am. You want to go with me?" There it was again. The words that just sprang from his lips without him even thinking them through. "I was planning on going once it warms up just a bit."

Annie chewed her lip. "Maybe. I'm usually pretty busy."

"A break might do you good." He was doing his best to convince her, and he wasn't even sure that's what he wanted. Of course, he wasn't sure about much of anything these days.

"Well, we can talk about it later." Annie seemed unwilling to commit.

"I was thinking I'd go up to the loft and work on some of the remodeling for you when I finish the coffee. What do you say?"

"You don't have to do that. You've probably already had a full day at work."

"It was a slow day. Just taught two classes. Couple of meetings. I have time. I'd like to help."

"Well, I try to keep the noise level down while the shop is open." Annie frowned. That darn frown of hers.

"I could prime the trim you want to put up."

"I… yes, that would be helpful."

Man, it was hard work offering to help Annie. Though, he knew her well. She didn't accept help often and probably wasn't thrilled about him helping her now. He took a last sip of his coffee and stood. "I'll just head on upstairs."

Annie came up to the loft about an hour later to check on him. "You doing okay?"

"Yep, found everything I need." He lifted another piece of trim up to rest on the two sawhorses so he could paint it.

"You can stop whenever you get tired."

He smiled at her. "Not tired. Not a bit."

"There you are." They both turned at the sound of a gruff and slightly out of breath voice at the top of the stairs.

"Mr. Dobbs." Annie hurried over to greet the man.

Old Man Dobbs. Now there was a name from the past. The man hadn't changed a bit. Surly scowl on his face. Worn slacks and a pull-over sweater. Round face that always glowed red. Nick slowly followed Annie over to where the man was standing looking around the loft.

Dobbs took a few steps into the area and paused when he saw him. "Nick Chambers?" Dobbs's face turned even redder if that were possible. "I thought you were long gone from this town."

"I'm back." Nick stood his ground.

"I see." Dobbs glowered at Nick and Annie with his famous scowl. "Well, I just came to see how the renovations are coming." He turned to Annie. "Do you have the proper permits for all of this?"

"I do. I turned in all the proper paperwork at city hall."

"Well, I'm just checking. We don't want people just building things that aren't up to code and such."

"Didn't know you worked for the planning commission." Nick took a step to stand beside Annie.

She put a hand on his arm and frowned at him.

"I... well, I don't. But I'm on the town council so of course, I like to keep up with all that's going on in town."

"I'm sure you'll find all of Annie's paperwork in order." Annie was that type of person. Played by the rules. Did things by the book. And Dobbs darn well knew that after all these years. He was just causing trouble, and Nick would have none of that. Dobbs didn't get to bully Annie, and he didn't like Dobbs's threatening tone of voice.

Annie took a step forward. "All the permits are on file, I assure you."

"Well, make sure all this passes inspection before it opens." Dobbs waved his hand then turned on his heels and tottered away to the stairs. He grasped the handrail as if convinced that Annie had put in the loft up all these stairs just to annoy him.

"Well, he hasn't changed." Nick turned to Annie.

"You didn't need to do that." Her eyes flashed.

"Do what?" His brow furrowed. What didn't he need to do?

"I can take care of this myself. You didn't need to step up and defend me."

"Annie… I…" She was right. He'd stepped in where he wasn't needed. "I just didn't like the way he was talking to you."

"I can take care of myself. I've been doing it for years without your help." Annie spun around and hurried back down to the shop.

CHAPTER 11

Nora handed Beth the container of cookies. "Here you go. The boys' favorite. Oatmeal."

"I don't know how you have time to run the lodge and bake for the boys. I can't seem to even have time to get our laundry done and keep the house from becoming a disaster zone." Her daughter grabbed her purse and juggled the tin of cookies. "I'm sure they'll be happy to see these. I can't tell you the last time I baked cookies for them. We're kind of in the fish sticks and store-bought snacks mode the last few weeks. I've got to get my act together and cook some healthy meals."

Dark circles etched their way under Beth's eyes, which meant that she wasn't getting enough rest. But her daughter had her hands full these days with her teaching job and the boys and all of their sports. Nora made a mental note to take the boys overnight again soon. Beth could use the break, and she enjoyed having her grandsons around.

"You let me know if there is anything I can do to help." She handed Beth a to-go mug of coffee.

"Mom, you already do so much for me."

Jason came walking in from the other room. "Sis, don't argue with your mother. Besides, you know she loves to help." He eyed her coffee mug. "How many of those have you had today?"

"Really, Jas? You, too? I'm doing the best I can."

"Wow, not criticizing. Teasing. I'm sorry." He lifted his hands in surrender.

"No, I'm sorry. I'm just tired and cranky today." Beth let out a long sigh.

"How about I pick the boys up from school tomorrow? I'll tire them out, take them out for burgers, and bring them home to you exhausted." He snatched an apple off the counter and took a big bite out of it.

Nora waited to see how Beth would respond

to her brother's offer. Her daughter didn't accept help often, which was part of the problem.

"You don't have to do that." Beth shook her head.

"I know I don't. I want to."

Beth paused, then nodded slowly. "Okay, thanks. That will let me get caught up on some things. I'll grocery shop too and get some food in the house that doesn't come from a can or a box."

"It's settled then." Jason smiled and walked out the door, crunching on his apple.

"I better go. Got to get the boys from sports practice and they still have homework to do."

"Try to get some rest." She opened the door for Beth.

"I'll try."

She watched as Beth climbed into her car and pulled away. Usually, her daughter managed to juggle all her responsibilities, but occasionally, when the boys' schedules got really crazy with sports, she struggled to do it all. If only her ex-husband would help more. But he was more of a come into town occasionally, spoil the boys with gifts, and depart again, leaving Beth with all of the day-to-day responsibilities. What Beth had ever seen in that man was beyond her. Well, okay, he'd been the star football player, handsome as all get-out, but he had no moral backbone and expected everything in life to come easy for him. Real parenting was just a bit too hard as far as he was concerned.

She turned to go back inside but paused at the sound of a car approaching. Annie waved as she pulled her car up to the cabin. Annie climbed out of the car and gave her a quick hug. "Got time for a cup of hot tea?" She linked her arm in Nora's.

"Always. I always have time for tea with you."

"Was that Beth I passed as I came in?"

"Yes. She was just leaving to go pick up the boys." Nora put the tea kettle on the stove and set out a plate of the oatmeal cookies.

Annie settled into her usual chair at the kitchen table. "I hear we're supposed to get a snow storm."

"I heard that, too. I'm ready for spring."

"I am, too. And I'm so over shoveling snow."

"I better be sure Jason has the blade on the tractor to clear the roads at the lodge."

Nora sat across from Annie and waited for the tea kettle to whistle. "So, what have you been up to? Things going okay with the remodel?"

"Yes, it's coming along. Nick's been a big help."

"I heard he went to dinner at your house."

Annie looked up in surprise, then smiled. "Not much gets past you."

"Not much. Did you have a good time?"

"We did. It's interesting getting to know Nick now. He's so different. He said he was looking into a research job."

Nora didn't like the way Annie's eyes lit up when she talked about Nick. Not one bit. "I thought he had a practice?"

"He does... or did. I don't know. He just said he wanted to try research now."

Nora got up and made their tea. As she sat back down, Annie leaned forward, her elbows on the table. "He came over yesterday, too. He went up to the loft to work and Dobbs came by."

Nora frowned. "What did Dobbs want?"

"He wanted to make sure I had all my permits for the remodel."

"Like that's any of his business."

"Then Nick kind of stood up to him and…" Annie sighed. "I don't need someone coming into my life and standing up for me. I've been fine on my own. I do appreciate the help with finishing the remodel, but he can't…"

"He can't come in and act like he's a part of your life again?"

"Well… yes. You're right. He was acting like he had to protect me or something. He just took over. Like I need protection from Dobbs. We dealt with him just fine with the whole pathway along the river, didn't we?"

"We did." Nora watched Annie's face. She knew her friend so well. She was struggling to figure out where Nick fit in her life now. As much as she wanted to tell her to just toss the man into the river, Annie was going to have to work things out on her own.

Nora just hoped Annie didn't get her heart crushed in the process.

NICK WALKED INTO BOOKISH CAFE, hoping Annie was still working. He needed to apologize. He'd overstepped with her yesterday, he'd figured that out. She was a capable woman, able to take care of herself.

It's just that his instincts had kicked in. All of a sudden, he was back in time. When Annie had relied on him, depended on him. They had depended on each other back then. When Dobbs had started in with his bullying, he hadn't been able to stop himself. And Annie had made it very clear that she could fight her own battles.

"Annie, there you are." He walked up to where she was stacking books on a table.

"Nick, you don't have to come here every day and work on the loft. It's my problem, not yours." She set down a pile of books with just a little too much force. They tumbled to the floor.

He bent to pick them up, but she put a hand on his shoulder. "No, I've got them." She bent down, gathered the books, and carefully placed them back on the table.

He waited for her to arrange them just so. Then change them a bit. Then again. She was stalling, he could see that. "Annie, I came to apologize. I overstepped yesterday. I know you can handle Dobbs. You've proven you're very capable. Look at all you've done with your life and this shop. I admit Dobbs has always gotten under my skin. He's just a pompous... well, a jerk. But I shouldn't have interfered."

Annie looked up at him. "I don't need you to stand up for me."

"I know I don't. I'm apologizing. Are you going to accept my apology?" He cocked his head to one side and grinned at her.

She tossed him a brief smile. "No need to apologize. I probably overreacted. I do that sometimes."

"Really?" He was sure she couldn't miss the sarcastic tone of his voice.

She smiled a full-out smile then. Finally. "Really. Only occasionally though."

"I remember." He could stand there all afternoon and bask in her smile. "Anyway, I came to ask you out to dinner. My way of saying I'm sorry."

"You don't have to do that."

"I know. But I want to. How about it?"

"No, I have so much that I need to do." Annie frowned.

Again with the frown. Bring back the smile.

"You have to eat sometime."

"I... do, but..."

"Great. Then I'll come by about six and

we'll walk over to Antonio's Cantina. Tell me it's still here."

"It is. Still the best Mexican food and margaritas in the state."

"Perfect. So we're on?"

Annie looked at him, and he could see the war going on in her sky-blue eyes. She finally shrugged. "You're right. I do have to eat, and I haven't been to Antonio's in forever."

Not the glowing, enthusiastic answer he was hoping for, but he'd go with it.

"I'll see you at six."

ANNIE COULDN'T SEEM to help herself. She'd never been able to say no to Nick's smile and charming ways. Anyway, a woman had to eat, right? Might as well share that meal with a friend.

A friend.

Is that what Nick was? What were they doing?

What was *she* doing?

She glanced at her watch, then out the shop window. A light snow was beginning to fall. She just hoped this would be the last one of the season. Soon the snow began to blanket the sidewalks. She stood in the window and watched as the evening sky darkened and the snow draped itself on the trees. She was so very tired of snow this year, but she had to admit it was beautiful.

The door to the shop opened and Nick entered. He stomped his boots to knock off the snow on the large mat by the front door. He looked up and saw her, and his face broke into a large smile. For a moment she was back in time, back when that smile was her whole world. Her heart fluttered in her chest, and she was fairly certain she didn't like that. Not one bit.

He crossed over to her, oblivious to her discomfort. "You ready to go?"

"I… ah… yes. Let me grab my coat."

They walked out into the crisp night air. The snow muffled the sounds and draped Main Street in an enchanting blanket of fresh snow.

"You want to walk?" Nick eyed her. "It's really pretty out. I haven't been out in snow in I don't know how long."

"Sure. Let's walk." They started down the block and crossed over to the side street to Antonio's Cantina. Cheerful Mexican music spilled through the doorway as they entered.

Antonio came over, and a wide smile spread over his face. He clapped Nick on the back and gave him a big bear hug. "Nicky. You're back."

Nick grinned. "I am. Good to see you, buddy."

"It's been a long time. But I knew my food would bring you back eventually." Antonio grinned.

"It sure did." Nick nodded. "Only reason I'm in town, of course.

"Come on you two. I'll get you your old table in the back. Margaritas for both of you? No salt, for you, right Annie?"

"Right."

CHAPTER 12

Nick held the chair for Annie to slip into it. At their same table in the same restaurant where they'd gone so many times. The past and the present wobbled together as he slipped into his own seat. Though this time he took the chair across from her, instead of right beside her like he always had before.

Soon he was sipping on the best margarita in the state. No lie.

They ordered their meals, and Antonio gave them a big order of nachos while they waited. Nick leaned on the table and reached for a chip. Annie reached at the same time and their fingers grazed. It took all of his control not to just take her hand in his.

But he didn't still have feelings for Annie.

Those were long gone, right? It had been years. He couldn't be having those feelings again. He'd only been back a short time. He hardly knew her anymore.

And yet... he wanted to take her hand in his.

Instead, he took the margarita in his hand, relishing the coolness of the glass, hoping it would quench not only his thirst but his... what? What was it that he was feeling for Annie?

He looked across the table at her, sitting there with a dazed expression on her face, which he was sure perfectly mirrored his own.

"What are we doing, Nick?" Her voice was low.

He wanted to act like he didn't know what she was talking about, but she could always tell when he wasn't telling the whole truth or was avoiding her question. "I'm honestly not sure."

"I'm not either. I don't think I can do this." She set her glass on the table.

"Do what? Be friends with me?"

"Is that what we are? Friends?"

A friend he had an overwhelming urge to kiss.

"I don't know, Annie. Can we just take it day by day? Not overthink things?"

"But I always overthink things." She gave him a weak smile.

"I know, but this once, let's just let it go. See where things head. I like spending time with you. I've missed talking to you. You're just so easy to talk to. Or even easy to work with side by side without talking."

Annie frowned, then quickly turned it into a smile when she caught herself. "Okay, we'll give it a try. *I'll* give it a try. But I don't make any promises on the overthinking thing."

THEY MANAGED to avoid any more talk about what they were or were not. Which suited Annie just fine. Though, she was determined to sit quietly at home later and try to sort things out, even if Nick didn't want her to. She had to figure out what she was doing... and if she wanted to be doing it. Whatever *it* was.

"Nick Chambers."

Annie looked up to see Gloria Edmonds standing by their table. Great, just great.

"Gloria." Nick looked up and smiled.

Annie wasn't sure she liked that.

"I heard you were back in town." Gloria

positively beamed at Nick, ignoring Annie completely. "It's *so* good to see you." She elegantly settled in the chair next to Nick. "I'd been hoping you'd stop by and see me."

"You have?" Nick's forehead creased.

"Well, of course. We were such good friends back in high school." Gloria flipped her obviously dyed hair over her shoulder.

The woman was *flirting* with him. Flirting. Annie seethed. "Gloria, we were just finishing up. Getting ready to leave."

"Oh, don't you want to stay and have one more drink with me?" She still never looked at Annie, but leaned closer to Nick. The woman had no shame.

"Ah, we're both driving, so we don't want to have another drink." Annie picked up her purse from the table.

"Well, that's too bad." Gloria rested her hand on Nick's arm. "We'll have to make it a point to get together while you're back in town."

Annie stood and grabbed her coat from the back of her seat, catching the chair right before it crashed to the floor.

"Um… sure." Nick looked uneasily from Gloria to Annie and stood up himself. "I guess we're leaving. Good seeing you."

"It was *great* seeing you, Nick. Don't be a stranger. You can always find me at Le Boutique on Main."

Annie was acutely aware the woman had still not said one word to her. "Bye, Gloria, enjoy your dinner." Not that she cared if the woman enjoyed it or not. She could choke on it for all she cared.

She was instantly appalled by her uncharitable thoughts. Even if they were mostly how she really felt...

"Well, Gloria Edmonds is still in town, huh?" Nick held the door open for Annie, and they slipped out into the wintery night.

"She'll never leave." Annie's voice held a tone he wasn't quite sure of.

"You and Gloria have some kind of run in?"

"You mean besides how she treated me in high school? Like I didn't exist? Or how about how she tried everything in her power to get Nora's husband—back when he was just Nora's boyfriend—to break up with Nora and go out with her?"

"Oh—"

"Or how she found out Nora and I were trying to get the river walk put in, and she did everything in her power to thwart us?" Annie pulled gloves out of her pocket and jerked them on her hands.

Nick paused under a streetlight, watching the anger chase across Annie's face.

"Or, how about… never mind. It doesn't matter. I just can't abide by that woman."

"I can see that." Nick figured he'd better take a wide berth around Gloria if he didn't want to run afoul of Annie and Nora. And he didn't. He wanted them both to like him again. Or at least not be mad at him. And preferably trust him.

He looked at Annie, her face tilted up to him, her eyes flashing. He took a deep breath and started to lean down toward her, toward her lips. He couldn't help himself.

Her eyes widened and she whirled away. "We should go. Look how much snow we've gotten already. It's really coming down."

What was he thinking?

He cleared his throat, shook his head, and trotted after Annie. "Wait up."

Annie slowed down her pace, and he caught up with her. She started to slip on the sidewalk, and he caught her gently by the arm. "Here, hold on. Looks like there's a layer of ice under this snow."

She rested her hand on his arm as they walked down the sidewalk. He pressed his hand over hers, trying to ignore the instant connection. But as far as he was concerned, they could walk on like this forever.

What was he doing?

All he knew was it felt right to be walking down the street in Sweet River Falls with Annie on his arm once again. Perfect and absolutely right.

CHAPTER 13

Annie could hardly breathe. She tried to convince herself it was because of the near miss on the slip on the ice, but she couldn't quite persuade herself to believe that lie. She knew it was because she was hanging onto Nick Chambers's arm. She felt like a young girl again.

His strong hand rested on hers, but she ignored it. Totally ignored it. They walked on in silence. The only sound she heard was the crunch of their steps on the snow-covered sidewalk. The wind had picked up and thrust the snow in a relenting sheet of icy darts. She bent her head against the onslaught.

"Here's my car." She stopped in front of her vehicle.

"Let me help you clear the snow off." Nick took his hand off hers.

The lack of connection to Nick threw her for a moment. She snatched her hand off of his arm and dug into her pocket for her keys. "You don't have to clear the car. You should get to your own car and get back to the lodge before it gets any worse." She opened the car and reached in for the ever-present snow scraper.

"Please. Hand me the scraper. You climb in and start the car and get it warmed up."

She handed him the scraper, secretly glad to be able to slip out of the wind. She slid the key in the ignition and turned it.

Nothing.

She frowned and didn't care who saw it.

She turned the key again. Just a faint tick, tick sound.

Nick tugged open the car door. "Sounds like your battery is dead."

"I've been meaning to replace it. Had to jump it the other day. Just haven't had time to get a new one." Annie wanted to bang her hands on the steering wheel but couldn't quite let herself express her frustration in front of Nick. It had been a careless choice to ignore the aging battery.

Nick held out a hand. "Come on. I'll drive you home. We'll deal with the battery in the morning."

She considered her choices. Get Nick to bring his car around and jump hers, all the while fighting the blinding snow, or let him take her home. Both were equally bad choices as far as she was concerned. Really bad choices. It had been so unsettling to have him back at the cabin this week. Besides, if he took her all the way to her place, he'd have to double back on the roads to get to the lodge.

"Come on, Annie. It's freezing out. Let me drive you home."

She took his outstretched hand and climbed out of her car. He kept his hand in hers, led her down the street, and helped her into his SUV. He climbed in and started the vehicle. A low light shone from the dashboard with a welcoming glow. She rubbed her arms, trying to get warm. She hadn't expected it to get this cold and had only worn a lightweight winter jacket.

"I'm going to clear the windows. Be right back." Nick slid out of the car, and a brief burst of cold air rushed in. She sat inside, watching the scraper slide across the windshield, glad she was inside while the car began to warm.

Nick popped back into the car, pulled off his gloves, and rubbed his hands together. "It's getting nasty out. Let's get you home all safe and warm."

She was ready for that. Ready to be home in her cabin and out of the storm. A crack of thunder boomed in the distance.

"Ah, a thundersnow storm. I'd forgotten that springtime sometimes brought with it the weird phenomena of thundersnow." Nick looked up at the sky. Or what they could see of it through the swirling snow.

"Which usually means we're going to get dumped on."

Nick pulled the car out, his headlights slicing through the snow. He slowly drove down the main street and took the road out of town toward the cabin. The snow swirled around, blanketing the road.

"Maybe we should turn around and head back into town. It's really getting bad out." Annie strained to see out the window.

"We're good. I'll just take it slow." His words were calm and reassuring.

They crept along the road while Nick carefully navigated the turns. After way longer than it should have taken, they were almost to the cabin. Her jaw ached from clenching her teeth. She peered outside as if to help Nick see better.

All of a sudden, a deer sprang in front of the car, illuminated by the headlights. A gasp escaped her lips. Nick swerved to avoid hitting the animal. "Hold on. Hold on." His terse voice cut through the darkness.

The car spun out of control, circling once, then sliding over to the edge of the snow-covered pavement. She watched in horror as they teetered on the edge then began sliding down the steep embankment at the side of the road. Each moment went by in slow motion. Tree branches snapped around them. Glass shattered. Her heart pounded so hard she couldn't catch her breath. She instinctively threw her hands up to protect her face.

After what seemed like an eternity, with a crunch of metal, they slammed to a stop.

Nick was out of his seat belt and leaning over her within seconds. "Are you okay? Annie?"

"I… I think so." She tried to clear her thoughts. She looked out in the darkness and saw two trees had miraculously stopped them from plunging the rest of the way down the hillside to the river below. The SUV hung between the two pine trees, balancing not quite completely on its side against them.

The windshield had cracked into millions of pieces, shattered around them. A tree branch poked through the opening. Her ankle hurt like all get out.

"Let's go. We need to get out. I'm not sure how long the trees are going to keep holding the car." Nick reached out his hand and climbed up the inclined car seat, pulling her with him. He wrestled the door open and climbed out. The car tilted crazily against the trees, but he firmly grasped her arms and pulled her to safety. They stumbled backward, and she crashed against his chest as they landed in the snow.

The car door slammed shut behind them. With a shudder, the SUV tottered and started to slide down the hill. Nick wrapped his arm around her and dragged them backward.

She watched in alarm as Nick's car disappeared down the slope. She held her breath until she heard a crash and a splash as it reached the bottom. Nick tightened his arm around her. "Sh. It's okay. We're okay. Everything is okay." His quiet litany did little to soothe her nerves.

She leaned against him and closed her eyes,

unwilling to follow the train of her thoughts on what could have happened to them. Her pulse raced, and her breath came out in ragged gasps.

"Can you walk? I need to get you out of this storm."

She opened her eyes. Nick's face was inches from hers, his eyes filled with concern. "I—I can walk." She could, couldn't she? She didn't think she was hurt that much, though her ankle throbbed.

"I think we're only about a quarter mile from the cabin. Let's go before you freeze." Nick stood up and pulled her unceremoniously to her feet. He wrapped an arm around her, and they slowly trudged back up the hillside to reach the road. The wind whipped the snow against her face as they fought their way along the road.

She was shaking with cold but ignored it, along with ignoring the pulsating pain in her ankle.

"You okay?"

"Yes." It was all she could do to get the one word out as they fought against the deepening snow and the fierce wind. Another crack of thunder rolled in the distance, promising more snow.

They finally reached the road to her house

and stumbled along the drive until she could see the porch light struggling to shine through the whiteout. Nick's strong arm still supported her every step of the way. She leaned against him, tired from the struggle, fighting the pain in her ankle, and exhausted by the pure terror of the crash.

ANNIE LEANED HEAVILY against him as they climbed the stairs to the front porch. He kept his arm firmly wrapped around her waist. The last few minutes of their trek he'd almost had to drag her through the snow. He needed to get her inside and warm.

"I don't have my key, it's in my backpack. Which must still be in the car." Her voice quavered.

"Which would be at the bottom of the ravine. Got a stashed key?"

"Yes-s-s-" Her teeth chattered. "By the back door, under the flower pot."

He didn't want to leave her, but they needed that key. Or he'd smash a window. One way or another he was getting her out of this storm.

But first, he'd look for the key. "Stay here. I'll be right back."

He fought his way through the drifting snow, ignoring the icy coldness that filled his boots, ignoring the bite of the wind. He struggled around to the back of the cabin and upended the flowerpot. After two attempts to pick up the key, he tugged off his gloves and retrieved it.

After several fumbled attempts with his frozen fingers, he managed to get the key in the lock. He pushed the door open and strode through the house, jerking the front door open as soon as he reached it.

Annie stood huddled beside the door. He reached out, wrapped an arm around her, and helped her inside.

The warmth of the cabin surrounded them. Annie flipped on the light and stood dripping snow onto the mat by the door.

"Come on. Let's get you out of these wet clothes. Get you warmed up."

She nodded, standing shaking before him. He berated himself for not taking her advice and heading back into town when she'd first suggested it to him. But no, he had to be the macho hero and drive her home.

Look how well that had worked out.

He unzipped her soaked jacket and let it slip to the floor. He gently pushed her into a chair by the door and knelt before her. He tugged off one of her boots. When he went to pull off her other one she winced.

"What's wrong?"

"I hurt my ankle."

His heart raced. She was hurt. He looked down to see his hands shaking. It was probably just from the cold…

He steadied his hands, removed the boot, and slipped off her sock. Her foot was icy cold and swollen. "Looks like you sprained it. We should get it looked at. Get an X-ray. Though I guess that's out of the question tonight. Why didn't you tell me? You walked all the way on it."

"What were our choices?" Her voice trembled.

"You should have told me." He would have carried her if need be. She must have been in a lot of pain tromping through that snow. She'd always been a stubborn, determined woman. He glanced up at her.

An ashen pallor covered her face. He didn't like the looks of it. Not at all. "You sit there. I'm going to start a hot shower for you. We'll get you all warmed up, then you'll sit and we'll prop up your foot."

She didn't argue with him for once.

"I'll be right back." He didn't like the constant tremors that raced through her body. Guilt washed over him. He caused this. It was his fault. He should have listened to her and turned back to town.

He hurried off and got the shower started, then helped her to the bathroom. "You going to be okay?"

"Yes, I've got it from here." Her teeth still chattered.

"I'm going out and bringing in some more wood for the fireplace. Just in case the electricity goes out."

"Then you need to come in and get out of your wet clothes. I still have some boxes of Dad's clothes in his closet that I've never gotten rid of." She paused and held onto the counter. "I'm sure you could find some sweats you can wear."

He hated to leave her here, so unsteady, but it wasn't like he could stay while she got in the shower.

"Okay. I'll get the firewood, then change. Now jump in the shower and get warmed up."

He backed out of the bathroom and pulled the door firmly shut behind him. He drew in a deep, exhausted breath, longing to sit down and get warmed up. But first he needed to bring in some loads of wood, then dry clothes, then make sure Annie was warmed up. Then he'd allow the exhaustion to take hold, but not before.

ANNIE limped out of the bathroom after a good long, hot shower. The shaking had somewhat subsided, though unsteadiness still flowed through her. Her ankle had settled down to a dull throb instead of a searing pain. She wanted nothing more than to sit on the couch, prop up her foot, and forget this evening had even happened. If she let her mind wander to the what ifs…

The spinning SUV. The teetering vehicle against the trees. The crash of the car as it hit the bottom and splashed into the river. They could have been in it. They could have…

She pushed the thoughts away and limped down the hallway. She heard sounds from her father's bedroom and slowly made her way to the open door. Nick stood in the low lamplight, a pair of her father's sweats resting on his waist, bare-chested, sorting through a box he'd set on the bed. She swallowed. She was the one who had told him to go rummage through her father's clothes. The boxes of clothes she'd just never been able to get rid of.

He looked up as she leaned heavily against the doorframe. "I hope it's okay. I grabbed a quick hot shower, too." His chest still glistened with drops of water. He grabbed the towel and rubbed his chest, then scrubbed the towel over his damp hair.

She limped over to the bed and dug through the box, handing Nick a plaid flannel shirt. "Here, this should fit." *Put it on. Cover your chest.* The chest she was doing her best not to stare at. He'd certainly kept himself in very fine shape over the years. She looked down at herself and her extra ten to fifteen pounds she could never quite lose the last few years. Aging didn't play fair with the sexes.

Nick tugged on the shirt and buttoned it up. "Here, let me help you. Let's get you out to the couch. I've made a fire."

She let him wrap his strong arm around her waist and help her over to the couch, forgetting all about her fierce I-can-do-it-myself independence, grateful for the help.

She sank onto the worn leather, glad to be off her foot. He grabbed an afghan off the back of the couch and settled it around her, his hand briefly grazing her cheek as he pulled the cover up under her chin.

"I'm going to put a pillow on the coffee table. Put your ankle up. I'll be back in a few minutes."

She did as she was told. The pain lessened a bit as she elevated her foot. A warm fire danced in the fireplace, casting a cozy glow in the room. She leaned back against the couch and adjusted the afghan around her.

She eyed Nick when he returned from the kitchen. "What's that for?" She looked at a plastic bag in his hand.

"It's an ice pack. We need to ice that ankle to keep down the swelling."

"You want me to put ice on my foot when I'm not even fully warmed up yet?" She narrowed her eyes.

"You really should. Found some ibuprofen in the cabinet. Brought you two. It will help with inflammation."

She couldn't decide if she was cross at him

or grateful. But ice on her ankle sure didn't sound very nice…

"Here, you can have this too." He handed her a glass. "Hot buttered rum. I would have made you hot tea, but I figured this is what you really need."

She reached for the drink and took a sip of the golden liquid. She sighed as a welcome warmth spread through her. The whole getting warm thing was interrupted when Nick unceremoniously peeled the afghan off of her foot and placed the ice pack on it. She grimaced.

He sat down beside her and slipped his arm around her shoulder. She resisted moving away, but only because the warmth of his body felt so nice against her. That was the only reason. For sure.

"You going to be okay?" His low voice wrapped around her like a beloved old quilt.

"I'm fine. Really. Getting warmed up, and my ankle is better now that I'm not walking on it."

"I still think you need to get it checked out."

He tightened his hold on her, and she couldn't help it, she leaned against him and closed her eyes. "I will."

The warmth and the sips of rum finally overcame her. Her last thought as she dropped off to sleep was how good it felt to be right here. With Nick. With his arm around her.

And she could have sworn she felt him kiss her forehead, but that was probably just a dream.

CHAPTER 14

nnie moved her head, drifting in the in-between stage of sleep and wakefulness. Her neck had a crick in it that finally coaxed her into opening her eyes. She looked right into the sleeping face of Nick Chambers. As she struggled to chase the sleep from her thoughts, she realized she was lying right up next to him, almost on top of him, cuddled up on the couch.

She started to pull away, and he tightened his arms around her, muttering something in his sleep. She held her breath, trying to think of how to extricate herself without waking him up.

He stirred slightly and opened his eyes part way. A lazy smile spread across his face. "Morning."

"Uh… morning." She started to pull away.

"Couple more minutes." He closed his eyes and his breathing steadied again.

How could he smile, talk, and fall right back asleep? She rested her head back on his shoulder and laid there listening to his breath, feeling his heart beating strongly against her. She should really get up. Maybe make some coffee. A couple more ibuprofen for her ankle would be a good choice too.

But still, she rested against him. The sounds of his breath and the beating of his heart lulled her back to sleep.

JASON HAD GOTTEN up at first light to start the long process of clearing the roadways and walkways at Sweet River Lodge. He jumped off the snowplow he'd been using to clear the roads at the lodge and grabbed a snow shovel. The storm had dumped so much heavy, wet snow. Roads around town were closed, and people staying at the lodge were sure to be headed for the dining room since no one was going anywhere right now. He needed to get the walkways cleared.

Trevor and Connor came racing up to him.

"Grams said we can play some outside, but we have to stay where she can see us. We're gonna build a fort."

"Sounds like a great idea."

"Good thing Momma let us stay here last night. It's more fun here when it snows." Connor threw his arms wide.

Jason looked up as a couple came out of a nearby cabin. A young boy raced excitedly back and forth along the edge of the driveway. The boy skidded to a halt as they approached.

"Morning." Jason nodded at them. "I'm still working at getting the walkways cleared."

"That's no problem." The man smiled at him. "We were going to get one last day of skiing in today, but it looks like that's not going to happen."

"Nope, the roads are pretty much shut down right now."

"Hey, you wanna help us build a fort?" Trevor looked at the boy.

"Can I?" The boy's eyes lit up. "We don't have snow on Belle Island. That's in Florida."

"I don't know." The woman looked uncertain.

"They'll stay within view of the lodge. I'll

keep an eye on them, and I'm sure my mom is watching, too."

"Please, Mom?"

"Okay. But stay with these boys and don't go where I can't see you from the dining lodge."

The boy turned to Trevor and Connor. "I'm Bobby. I just learned to ski. This is my new stepdad, AJ. He taught me. I was really good at it, wasn't I, AJ?"

The man laughed. "You were, Bobby."

"I'm Connor, and this is Trevor. So you don't have any snow where you live?"

"Nope. And snow is like the best thing ever." The boy danced from foot to foot in his obviously new snow boots.

"Come, let's go get started." Connor raced off to a spot near the entrance to the dining lodge with Trevor and Bobby scrambling to keep up with him.

The man turned to him and reached out a gloved hand. "We're the Hamiltons. AJ and Courtney."

Jason took the man's hand. "Glad to meet you. I'm Jason Cassidy."

"So Nora is your mom?" Courtney asked. "We met her when we checked in."

"Yep. She is. Those two rascals are my nephews."

"Well, it looks like Bobby is having fun even if we couldn't make it to one last day of skiing. What do you say, Courtney? Want to go get some hot coffee and breakfast now?" The man took the woman's hand in his.

She took one more look at the boys and smiled up at AJ. "I do."

AJ laughed and leaned down and kissed her quickly. "You've gotten pretty good at saying those words since the wedding."

She laughed. "I guess I have."

Jason watched as the couple headed to the dining lodge. Courtney held onto AJ's arm as they navigated the snowy path. AJ said something to Courtney, and she threw back her head and laughed, the sweet tones of it drifting back toward him in the crisp air.

He turned back to the job at hand, thrust the shovel into the snow, and tossed the wet snow off of the pathway.

NORA LOOKED up as Jason walked through the door to the lodge, stamped the snow from his boots, and crossed over to the reception desk.

"I've got the road to the lodge plowed, not that the main road is cleared, but I still need to finish shoveling the walkways." He grabbed a coffee mug from the sidebar near the reception area and filled it from the always-waiting coffee urn.

"I'm worried about Annie. I can't get ahold of her." Nora stared at her cell phone again as if that would make her friend magically call.

"Probably just bad cell service." He wrapped his hand around the warm mug.

"She's not answering her house line either." She frowned. It wasn't like Annie not to check in after a storm. They had an agreement. She worried about Annie ever since she'd moved to the cabin and lived out there all alone.

"Maybe the house phone is out, too? That was quite a storm we had." Jason took a sip of the hot coffee, still cradling the mug in his hands. His cheeks were red from the wind, and his hair was tousled.

She wished he'd wear a hat when it was this cold, but he rarely did. Her mothering failure, or his stubbornness, she wasn't sure which.

She walked over to the window and checked on the boys "Looks like they made a new friend."

"Yep, Bobby. He and his folks are staying here. AJ and Courtney Hamilton.

"Oh, they are in having breakfast now. They seem like a nice couple. They already said they had plans to come back here again next year."

He laughed. "You turn just about everyone into a repeat customer, don't you?"

"I try." She stepped away from the window. "I am worried about Annie though. I called the shop and Lindsey answered and said Annie wasn't in yet, which is unusual."

"Maybe she can't make it out of her drive. We really got hammered with snow last night. These spring storms can be brutal."

"Lindsey said Annie's car was still parked outside the shop. Maybe I'll walk over to Nick's cabin and see if he knows where she is."

"No need. His SUV isn't there. No tracks. I don't think he made it back here last night."

"So maybe she's with him? Maybe he drove her home?" Nora didn't like the sound of that, because if he drove Annie home and he wasn't back here at the cabin, it probably meant he was still with her?

And what did that *mean* exactly?

"Jason, I hate to ask you this, but could you take the snowmobile over the ridge to her cabin and check on her? I'd do it myself, but I'm dealing with panicked people who can't get out today and a bunch of cancellations from people who can't get here for the weekend." Annie's cabin was a bit of a drive by road, but not very far over the ridge. There was a small footbridge over Ponderosa Creek where Jason could cross.

"Sure. I'll do that if it will make you feel better. I know you worry about Annie out there alone."

She was actually more worried about Annie out there with *Nick* right now...

Jason took one more long swig of coffee and set the mug on the counter. "I'll call as soon as I find out anything. I told the Hamiltons I'd keep an eye on the boys, though."

"I'll watch them. Thanks, Jason."

Nora kept busy with people trudging into the lodge for breakfast with questions about the roads and answering calls from other people wondering if they'd be able to make it in for their weekend reservations. She glanced at the clock in the lobby yet again. She pulled out her cell phone to make sure she hadn't missed a call from Jason.

Finally, her phone rang, and she snatched it off the reception desk. "Jason?"

"Mom... I... uh..."

"Tell me." She didn't like Jason's tone of voice.

"Well, I've found Nick's SUV. It's... it's at the bottom of a ravine, partially submerged underwater."

"What?" Her pulse raced and she reached up to rub her temple.

"There's no one in the SUV. But, Mom? I can see the path where it slipped down the hillside. Lots of broken trees and branches."

"But no sign of Nick or Annie?"

"I... uh."

"Jason, just tell me."

"Well, I found Annie's backpack at the side of the stream. I already called the sheriff. I'm going to head to Annie's now, and if she's not there, I'll start looking. The sheriff said they're backed up with emergencies and calls."

"I'm coming over." Nora looked around in a panic, trying to remember where she put her coat.

"No, don't. The roads are terrible. Let me

go check. I'll call you as soon as I get to her cabin."

"Thanks, Jason." Nora clicked off her phone, still not certain that she shouldn't just get in her car and head over to Annie's, but Jason was probably right. The roads would be nearly impassable for a while until the plows could get out and get things cleared.

Annie.

Where was she? Was she okay? Nora's heart squeezed in her chest. She couldn't bear to think of Annie stuck out in the storm… or worse.

NICK WOKE up to a tingling sensation in his arm. He slowly opened his eyes and let his mind process where he was. It felt familiar, yet foreign.

At Annie's.

He glanced down at her sleeping soundly beside him. He wanted to move his arm to relieve the pins and needles tormenting him, but he couldn't bear to wake her. The corners of her mouth turned up in the tiniest of smiles, and she sighed in her sleep. He tightened his hold of her, thankful she was okay after last night's ordeal.

He peeked over and saw the fire had died down to just a few embers. The cabin had cooled off substantially. Maybe the electricity had gone off. He scanned the room for any sign that would tell him the electricity was on or off.

Nothing.

The sound of a snowmobile closing in on the house made him stir and try to slip his arm from around Annie. He still needed to get her to town and get her ankle checked. If people were out on snowmobiles, maybe he could flag someone down for help. Annie murmured in her sleep and curled up on the couch as he carefully sat up.

At the sound of pounding at the door, Annie's eyes flew wide open. He quickly stood. "I'll get it."

He crossed to the door and tugged it open.

"Nick. You're okay."

Nora's son stood in the doorway. What was his name?

Annie limped up behind him. "Jason, come in."

Jason, that was it.

"I came over the ridge to check on you. Mom was worried. I found Nick's car at the bottom of the ravine. Are you okay?"

141

"I'm fine. Just hurt my ankle a bit."

Jason entered the cabin, and Nick closed the door behind him. "We need to get Annie into town to get her ankle checked out."

"The roads aren't cleared yet but should be soon. I'd take her on the snowmobile, but it's a pretty rough ride."

"I'll wait."

Nick paused, considering the options. "But we don't have a car here to bring you to town."

"I'm sure Mom can come get you as soon as it's clear. I'll call my friend, Gabe. He's got his plow out working with the road crew. I'll have him let me know when the road is clear here. And I'll have him come plow your drive, too. We'll get you to town as soon as we can."

"It's not an emergency or anything. I'm fine."

"Look at your ankle." Nick eyed Annie's foot.

"Oh."

Her foot was swollen and purple. He crossed over and wrapped an arm around her waist. "Back to the couch. You should stay off of it."

He got her settled on the couch. "I'm going to make coffee. Jason, you want some before you head out?"

"That sounds, great." Jason shrugged off his jacket. "I better call Mom and let her know Annie is okay."

Jason called Nora and after talking to her, handed the phone to Annie. "Mom wants to talk to you. I think she just needs to hear your voice to believe me that you're really okay."

"Nora, I'm fine. No really. I am." Annie leaned back on the couch and held the phone up to her ear.

Nick smiled and headed to the kitchen to make the much-needed coffee.

CHAPTER 15

Annie clumsily maneuvered the sidewalk with her crutches and entered Bookish Cafe with Nora hovering at her side. "Nora, I'm fine. Really. You heard the doctor. It's just a sprain. He's got it all wrapped up."

"You shouldn't be working. You should be home resting."

"I'll sit behind the register." Annie wasn't going to admit to Nora that her ankle was throbbing again, nor did she have any plans on taking the pain pills the doctor had prescribed.

"I wish you'd go home. I'll take you."

"I'm fine."

Nora scowled. "Well, I'm coming back about four and bringing you back to my cabin for the night. I don't want you out there alone, hobbling around."

"I'll get my car fixed and drive myself back to my cabin. I'll be okay."

"You hurt your right foot. You're not driving."

Annie sunk onto the stool, leaned her crutches against the counter, and looked at her foot. Nora was right. She wasn't going to be able to drive until her foot got a little better. "Okay, I'll take a ride. But can you bring me back to my cabin? I just really want to stay there."

Nora sighed. "There is no use arguing with you. Okay, I'll take you home. But I'm going to bring something for your dinner and you have to promise me you'll try and stay off your foot."

Annie smiled at her friend. She'd be the exact same way if Nora was hurt. "Okay, I promise. Now you get back to the lodge. I'm sure you have a ton of work to do. I've taken up too much of your time. But thank you for dropping Nick off at the car rental and taking me to the doctor."

"I thought I'd have to physically throw him out of the car to keep him from going to the doctor with you." Nora rolled her eyes.

"He was acting a bit overprotective." Annie smiled.

"A *bit*? Well, that's one way to put it." Nora tugged on her gloves and turned to Lindsey. "Make sure she takes it easy. Call me if you think I should come get her."

"Hey, I'm sitting right here." Annie tapped on the counter.

"But I trust Lindsey's judgment more than yours." Nora gave a small wave and walked out of the door.

NICK PULLED his rental car up to his cabin. The road to the lodge had been cleared. He wanted to get cleaned up then go into town and check on Annie. He'd called her and she'd said the ankle was sprained, but she was fine. She was at work, of all things. The woman did not know how to take it easy.

Jason was hard at work a few cabins over, shoveling the pathway. He was torn between heading inside so he could ask how Annie was doing and helping Jason with the snow. Jason had come and rescued them after all. Duty won out and he headed over to where Jason was working.

"Got another one of those snow shovels?"

Jason looked up. "You don't have to do that."

"I want to."

"Well, I'm not going to say no twice. There's another shovel leaning against the snow plow over there on the road." Jason pointed to the plow.

Nick grabbed the shovel and started in. Before long, he was hot and sweaty. He'd forgotten what hard work it was shoveling wet spring snow. They kept at the chore until every cabin had been cleared and they ended up at the lodge.

"I really appreciate the help." Jason leaned his shovel against the railing and stretched his arms out.

"It was no problem." Except that every muscle in his body was screaming at him.

"Come in for some coffee. Get warmed up."

"I'm plenty warm, but I will take some coffee." They climbed the stairs to the porch and went inside.

Nora stood behind the reception desk, a frazzled look on her face. "Yes, I'll cancel your reservation. No, we don't have any openings for next week. I know. Yes, that's too bad. Well, we hope you can make it here soon." She set down the phone. "So many calls today and changes to reservations."

Jason walked over to the coffee urn and poured two steaming mugs. "Nick helped me clear all the pathways to the cabins."

"Nick, you didn't need to do that." Nora scowled.

What she meant to say was thanks for helping. He was sure that's what she meant... "It was no problem. Glad to help." He walked over and took the mug, not sure if he was ever going to win Nora over to his side again.

"I'm just getting ready to go pick up Annie and take her home. I'm sure she's exhausted by now even though she won't admit it." The phone rang and Nora turned to answer it. "Just a minute. I'll see if we have any openings that weekend."

He and Jason lounged against the reception desk as Nora clicked on the computer. As soon as she hung up, it rang again. She swiped the phone off the hook and answered.

Three young boys came racing in from the

snow. "Uncle Jason. You should see the fort we made."

The boys tugged off their caps, and Nick looked into the startling blue eyes of one of the younger boys. For a moment he was back in time. He closed his eyes for a second, trying to regain his balance, refusing to accept the similarities. He sucked in a deep breath to steady himself.

"These two monsters are my nephews. Connor and Trevor." Jason grinned.

"I'm Trevor." The one blonde-haired boy reached out his hand. "And this is our new friend, Bobby."

Nick's hand trembled as he forced himself to shake the boy's hand. He looked so like...

No, put that thought away.

"You coming, Uncle Jason?" The boys turned around to head back outside, a whirlwind of energy.

"Be there in a sec." Jason turned to him. "They're a handful. Don't know how my sister keeps up with them. I better go see this incredible snow fort."

Nick was just thankful they'd gone back outside. Not that they seemed like bad kids. But the one boy was just—

Nora hung up the phone, pulling him away from memories he didn't want to think about much less dwell on. Nick set his mug on the counter. "I can see you're busy. Let me go pick up Annie for you."

"No."

"Mom, you *are* busy. Let Nick do it. I swear you never accept help. Neither does Beth." He turned to Nick and let out a long-suffering sigh, then grinned. "See what I have to put up with?"

"Nora, it's no trouble. That is if Annie will ever ride in a car with me again."

"I don't know…" Nora's eyes clouded with doubt.

"Mom, let him. I'll help you here. We'll get all the reservations sorted out and we'll be able to help with dinner at the lodge. I doubt if many of our guests are headed into town for dinner."

"Okay." Nora agreed but didn't look happy. "I've got her dinner wrapped up in the kitchen."

"I'll get that then head out." Nick hurried out before Nora could change her mind. He grabbed the meal—enough to feed an army— headed to his cabin, took a quick shower, changed clothes, and headed into town. He couldn't wait to see with his own eyes that Annie was okay.

~

ANNIE LOOKED AT HER WATCH. Nora would be here soon. She didn't want to admit it, but she was tired. Really tired. Her ankle hurt more than ached, and she was wavering on her plan to avoid the pain pills.

The door to the shop opened and Nick walked in. She smiled at him automatically before she could even think about it. He smiled back at her, and the world faded away for the briefest of moments.

"What are you doing here?" She stood and balanced against the counter.

"I came to pick you up. Nora got tied up with work. That's okay with you?" He looked at her.

"Of course."

"You're not afraid of riding in a car with me again?" He narrowed his eyes.

"Of course not. It was an accident. It could happen to anyone. Natural reaction to swerve to avoid hitting the deer."

"Well, I missed the deer, but the rest of it was rather… unfortunate."

"It was. But we're okay. So what did the car rental agency say?"

"Lots of paperwork. Kind of surprised they rented to me again…"

"Accidents, Nick. They happen." She reached for her crutches and turned to the woman behind the counter. "Lindsey, I'm leaving."

"It's about time." Lindsey shook her head. "And I'm opening in the morning, so don't you come rushing in tomorrow, either. You're supposed to take it easy." Lindsey turned and started to walk away. She paused and added, "Or you'll have to answer to Nora. Nobody in their right mind crosses Nora."

Annie laughed. "We'll see." She wasn't about to commit to coming in late to work. She leaned on her crutches.

"Can I help you?" Nick hovered near as she came out from behind the counter.

"No, I've got it." She wobbled over to the door with Nick right at her side.

They went out to his car, and he helped her inside and tossed her crutches in the back seat. He slid in beside her and turned on the car. "All set?"

"I'm good." Or she was crazy. Trapped in a car with Nick once again…

They headed out of town on those same

roads they'd taken last night. They didn't look nearly as menacing as yesterday. The sun shone brightly, and the workers had done a good job clearing the main roads.

When they got to the part of the road where their car had slid off last night, she looked and saw Nick's knuckles were white from gripping the steering wheel. She held her breath as they passed safely by the site and continued on to her cabin.

Nick got out and grabbed her crutches. She climbed unsteadily up the stairs with him right by her side, his hand inches from her back, ready to catch her if she stumbled.

She handed him her key while she balanced on her one good foot and the crutches. The whole maneuvering through the door was awkward, and she bumped against his chest. He caught her arm and steadied her. "You okay?"

"Yes, of course," she snapped. A long sigh escaped her. "I'm not very graceful on these things, and I'm tired. Sorry to be so cranky."

"Hadn't notice." He tossed her a smile. "Why don't you sit? I'll start the fire and make you some tea."

As much as she hated being waited on, she was grateful for the help. She hobbled over to the couch and sank down on it, thankful for its welcoming comfort and glad to be off her foot.

"Prop your foot up." He nodded at her. "I'll get more firewood."

He headed out the back door as she shrugged out of her coat and did as he asked. She carefully set her foot on a throw pillow on the coffee table and leaned back. She still debated on taking a pain pill but decided all she really needed was to stay off her foot for a bit and rest. The warmth of the cabin and the comforting sounds of Nick puttering around in the kitchen lulled her to sleep.

She awoke with a start, surprised to see it was dark outside. The flames from the fire tossed cheerful flickers of light around the room.

"Morning." Nick sat in the recliner beside the couch.

She rubbed her eyes. "How long was I asleep?"

"Couple of hours."

"You didn't need to stay."

"I wanted to. I don't like you being here alone and on the crutches. You're... well, let's just say your talents lie somewhere else than using those crutches."

"Gee thanks." She knew she was an accident

waiting to happen on those crutches, but she could be careful and manage in her own cabin.

No stairs. She'd be fine.

She grabbed the crutches leaning against the couch to prove her point and hoisted herself up. Nick was up in an instant and by her side. Which was a good thing because she totally lost her balance and went tumbling sideways. He wrapped his strong arm around her and held her close.

"Like I said. I didn't want to leave you here alone on your crutches."

He still held her close. Her breath came out in ragged gasps... probably from the near fall. Not because she could feel his heartbeat and his breath was warm against her forehead.

"You win. I'll accept your help. I am pretty lousy on these things. I'll get better."

"I'm sure you will. Now, why don't you sit? I'll reheat the tea and I have the dinner Nora sent warming in the oven."

He took her crutches and helped her settle back on the couch. Like a cold blast of air, all contact with him was gone as he took his hands away and headed to the kitchen.

She watched each step he took as he walked away. The worn floor creaked under the rhythmic thunk of his boots. She'd missed that. The sound of a man walking through this cabin with boots. Who knew a person could miss a simple sound so much?

She wanted to leap up and follow him. Lounge in the kitchen and talk and laugh like they used to. But there would be no leaping in her near future.

CHAPTER 16

Nick leaned against the counter, steadying himself. His pulse raced and his heart pounded. He grabbed a glass and poured himself some cold water, which he finished in just a few large gulps. He wanted nothing more than to stride back into the family room and take Annie into his arms.

He'd spent a solid hour watching her sleep after he'd made the fire. Sitting and staring at her. He'd watched her grimace in pain when she moved her ankle, and it had taken all his willpower not to go over to that couch and gather her in his arms. He'd watched, fascinated as her lips moved slightly as if she were talking to someone in her dreams. He'd stared at the firelight dancing across her face, curling his fists into balls to keep from leaning over and brushing a lock of her soft blonde hair away from her forehead.

Ah, Annie. What had she done to him now?

He shook his head, chasing away the thoughts. He needed to get dinner finished. That would be something he could focus on.

He methodically set the table, taking way more time than it should take and putting way more effort into it than it needed. He finally took the food out of the oven. A healthy portion of beef stew, rolls, and an apple pie. Nora did nothing halfway. He poured hot water for their tea and surveyed the room.

Then he realized the fatal flaw to his plan.

He was going to have to go back out and get Annie off the sofa and into the kitchen. He'd have her in his arms again.

Which really wasn't a very good idea.

Or was it?

He scrubbed his hand over his face and turned slowly around to face her. He walked out into the family room and reached down his hands. "Ready for dinner?"

She placed her small hands in his, and he effortlessly pulled her to her feet. She leaned against him while she adjusted her crutches just so. Her hair smelled faintly of lilacs. Her face contorted in concentration as she moved the crutches. They slowly made their way into the kitchen, and she settled into her chair. He could finally step away from her and catch his breath.

"Wow, Nora sent enough to feed ten of me."

He slipped into his chair, safely on the other side of the table. "Or feed you *and* me."

She smiled. "Or that."

They fell silent as they ate their meal. He wanted to talk to her, ask her a million questions about her life since he'd been gone. But that always brought them back to the fact he'd left…

"Nora's a great cook, isn't she?" She looked at him as she reached for a piece of the apple pie.

"She is."

"She learned to cook huge amounts of food when she had to do all the cooking for the lodge. Now she has a cook, but she used to do almost everything there."

"She and her husband split? I mean I've met her kids but haven't seen any glimpse of a husband."

"He's… gone. He died when the kids were small."

"Oh, I'm sorry."

Annie nodded. "I'm sorry, too. It's been rough on Nora. They had just bought the lodge. Only had it a few years before he passed away. After he died, she threw herself into the lodge. Building a few more cabins when she had a good year. Rehabbing the older ones. I helped with some of that. So did Dad while he was still alive."

So Nora was just as hard a worker as Annie and had done most of it on her own. Both the women impressed the heck out of him.

Here he was hiding out with his safe little teaching job. He really should make a note to call the research center in Houston about the job he'd applied for and see where they were on hiring decisions. He could still make a difference, help find some cures or ways to lessen the pain. He could at least do that.

Annie, oblivious to his self-chastising thoughts, handed him a piece of pie. "Nora's husband died of cancer. He found out he had it and within a year was gone. It was very sad."

He didn't even know what to say to that. He'd think, being a doctor and being around death so much, he'd know what to say. But he didn't.

"Anyway, it's been over twenty years now

that he's been gone. A lifetime, really. Nora has managed to find a life on her own. Well, she has the kids, of course. Though they are grown and have their own lives."

"Jason works at the lodge full time?"

"He does. He got a business degree in hotel management and came back to work with his mom. He seems to love it. He's a whiz with numbers and really helped turn the lodge around. They've been able to do a lot of things to update it, but still keep the rustic vibe it has."

"It really is a beautiful property."

"It is. Just wait until it warms up. Nothing nicer than sitting on one of those benches by the stream or going out to sit by the lake and watch the sunrise. So beautiful."

He'd like to do just that, but he'd like to do it with Annie...

She put down her fork. "It's getting late. I should help you clean up these dishes. You don't need to be hand washing dishes because I don't want a dishwashing machine."

"Nope. I've got them. You go back and sit by the fire."

"I can't just sit."

He grinned at her. "I remember that about you, too. Let me help you back to the sofa, and we'll find you a crossword puzzle to do. You still do those, don't you?"

"I do."

～

ANNIE LET Nick help her get settled back on the couch. He stoked the fire and went back into the kitchen. She could hear him rattling around in there, cleaning up. She wasn't used to people waiting on her. She didn't think she liked it much. She liked to be self-sufficient and do things for herself.

But the sprained ankle had really cut into that. She should just sit back and let him help.

She reached over and picked up the crossword puzzle and started in. Playing with fire. Nine letters.

Dangerous.

Very funny, universe. I hear you. I'll be careful.

Nick came out of the kitchen with two glasses of wine. "I thought you might like one?"

"That sounds great." She reached for the glass, careful not to brush his fingers, not to touch him.

He sat next to her on the sofa, and that ruined the not touching thing. He settled back, oblivious to her desire to scoot just a few inches away from him. Though she'd probably look like an awkward fool maneuvering away with her hurt foot.

She wanted to lean back on the couch, but Nick had his arm casually draped across the back of it. If she leaned back, she'd be right in his arms.

He looked at her and laughed. "Relax. You can lean back. I promise I won't bite."

She slowly did as he said and relaxed against his arm. Suddenly the world seemed to fall into place. Everything felt right and perfect. Here with Nick, sitting by the fire, his arm around her.

No matter what the crossword puzzle had warned her.

She turned to look at him and saw the fire burning in his eyes. He reached his hand over and tilted her face up. Her heart pounded, and her lips parted. He leaned in and pressed the gentlest of kisses against her lips.

"Ah… I've wanted to do that since I first saw you on campus." His low voice lured her, wrapping her in its seductive charm.

Emotions rolled through her. Panic, need, fear, want. "I'm not sure this is smart…"

"I think—I think it's the smartest thing I've done in years." He leaned over and kissed her again. This time taking his time until she was breathless and clung to the front of his flannel shirt.

He started to pull back, and she stopped him, pulling him closer. He deepened his kiss.

This. This is what she'd been missing for so many years. Nick's company. Talking to Nick. Sharing with Nick.

Nick's kisses.

He pulled away and trailed a finger along her cheek. "I've missed you."

"I've missed you, too."

"I'm so glad I took this job at Mountain Grove. I'm even glad we had the storm so we could spend so much time together." He touched her lips. "But I am sorry you got hurt."

She tried to concentrate on his words, but mostly her mind demanded to know where he would touch her next.

He pulled his hand away and tucked her against his side. She had to keep herself from reaching up and stroking her lips where his fingers had just burned a trail.

She was probably a crazy woman for letting

him kiss her, but she was certain nothing could have stopped it.

She'd wanted it.

He'd wanted it.

She'd *needed* it.

And she wasn't sure she liked needing anything from Nick Chambers.

NICK WAS certain he could just sit here with Annie tucked up against him for the rest of the night. Or forever. Whichever came first. All his feelings that he'd stashed away when he'd left. The assurances he was making the right decision leaving all those years ago. Those decisions were mocking him now.

He could have had this.

But he gave it all away to follow his career.

His mess of a career.

He stifled a sigh so Annie wouldn't pick up on his confusion. She leaned against him, staring into the fire and absent-mindedly trailing her fingers up and down the skin on his arm where his shirt was rolled up.

Her touch seared him, and he wanted to

clamp his hand over hers and stop her. But he didn't.

She stirred, leaned forward, and turned to look at him. "It's getting late. You should probably head back. You don't want to be out very late on these roads in case they freeze up again."

"I don't want to leave you here."

"I'll be fine." Annie's words were firm.

He didn't like leaving her here, but he knew how she was when she set her mind on something. "How about I stay until you get ready for bed and I know you're safely tucked in your bed?"

She rolled her eyes at him. "If it makes you feel better."

She got up from the couch and grabbed her crutches. This time she safely maneuvered her way around the coffee table and headed down the hall. "It won't take me long. Then you can head out."

Nick placed his hand on the sofa beside him, still warm from the heat of her sitting there. What was he doing? Not that he was able to stop himself. Something was drawing him back into Annie's life, under her spell.

He let out a low groan. Instead of the simple

time he'd planned with his escape to his safe teaching job… he was getting a big serving of complications.

He jumped up at the sound of Annie's scream and a crash coming from her bedroom. He rushed into her room and found her lying on the floor. "Are you okay?" He scanned her quickly with the instinct of many years of medical practice.

"I'm fine. Just embarrassed." She reached up and touched the back of her head. "Ouch."

"You're hurt."

"Just hit my head a bit."

"Let me see."

He helped as she struggled to sit up. He looked at her head. It wasn't cut, but she was going to have a good-sized bump on it. Then, of course, he was going to worry because she'd hit her head. "Do you feel dizzy?"

"Nope. Just silly."

He cradled her tightly against him. "You scared me."

"Hey, I scared *me*."

"Listen, I know you want me to leave, but I really, *really* want to stay. I'll sleep on the couch. You just call me if you need me."

Her blues eyes looked up at him, and he

could see her determination waver. "I'll worry all night if I leave. Won't get a wink of sleep." He brushed a lock of her hair away from her face.

She let out a long sigh. "Okay. But we're not going to make this a habit. I'll get better with these crutches soon, and the doctor said I'd probably only need them a few days or so."

He reached out and touched her chin. "Thanks, Annie." He gathered her into his arms and with one swoop stood. He carefully placed her on the bed. "There."

"Thanks. I'll be fine now." She scooted under the covers.

He settled the quilts around her. "I know you will be. But call if you need me. I'll just be out on the couch."

"I feel bad that you're sleeping on the couch." A frowned crossed her face. "You could sleep in Dad's room."

"The couch will be fine." The last place he wanted to sleep was her father's room. Where he wanted to sleep was right beside her, making sure she was safe. He backed away before his resolve weakened and he kissed her again.

"Goodnight, Annie." He switched off the light.

"Night, Nick."

He walked back out to the family room and stretched out on the couch. He punched a throw pillow into comfortable submission and tugged the afghan over him. He watched the flames dance in the slowly dying fire. His muscles screamed at him for all his snow-shoveling good deeds today.

So much had happened since he'd returned to Colorado. Seeing Annie. Becoming friends again, and maybe more. Kissing her tonight had been so right.

But what was he doing? What were *they* doing? He was only here for a short time, then he'd be off, hopefully to a new research job. It's not like there were research jobs in his field in Sweet River Falls.

And as much as it pained him to think about it, he was pretty sure history was going to repeat itself. He was going to go off to follow his career, and Annie would be left behind.

If they continued on like this, he was going to hurt her again. And that was the last thing in the world he wanted to do.

Those kisses they'd shared tonight, they'd be the last ones. He'd talk to Annie in the morning.

Annie looked down at Nick sleeping on her couch. He must have been exhausted because he hadn't stirred when she'd clumped to the kitchen and made coffee. The morning sunlight streamed through the window and fell across his brown hair. A few strands of gray were threaded through his thick, wavy locks, and his temples were slightly gray. Yet, in his sleep, he looked so like the boy she'd been so in love with.

But this was now. She wasn't in love with him. She wasn't going to make that mistake again.

Nick stirred in his sleep and opened his eyes. He smiled at her. "Morning."

"I made coffee if you want some. I would have brought you a cup, but I figured just walking around with these crutches was about the best I could do. Couldn't juggle a cup, too."

He sat up and stretched. As much as she tried, she couldn't take her eyes off of him. Here. In her cabin.

"You okay? You have this weird look on your face."

She steadied herself on her crutches, her

knuckles white on the handles. "Nick, we can't do this."

He looked directly at her and started to speak, but then closed his mouth. He nodded slowly.

"Last night... the kiss. The kisses. They were a mistake. We can't go down that road again. *I* can't."

He let out a long, drawn-out sigh. "I know. I agree with you. Kind of. It's just..." He ran his hand through his hair. "I've missed you."

Her determination crumbled at his words. *He'd missed her.* But that didn't change things. She gathered her courage. "I've missed you too, but it doesn't change the fact that you're leaving soon. You have your career. I belong in Sweet River Falls."

He looked down at his hands, straightened his shirt, then twisted his watch back into place on his wrist. When he looked back up at her, a sadness lurked in his eyes. "But we can still be friends, right? I still want to help you with remodeling your shop."

She wanted to say no to that. She wanted to say they couldn't even be friends. But she'd missed his friendship. She needed his help with the remodel, especially after messing up her foot.

And if she was honest with herself, she wasn't willing to give up all contact with him now that he was back. Not yet.

Which was probably dangerous, but she couldn't just not see him while he was so near.

"Yes, we can be friends. But friends only. No more... well, nothing more than that. And I do appreciate you helping me with the remodel."

"Okay, then we're agreed. And we are a pretty good team at construction work." Nick rose from the couch. "Now, let's have some of that coffee, and when you're ready, I'll drive you into town."

Annie was glad they'd gotten all that settled. Friends. Just friends.

Then why did a wave of sadness flow through her? It was what she wanted, right?

CHAPTER 17

Annie couldn't remember ever feeling this alive. Every moment seemed precious. Now that they'd cleared the air and were resolute in their decision that they'd only be friends, she could relax and just enjoy Nick's company.

He came over almost every evening to work on the shop. She was pretty sure they were going to have it finished before the May Festival. At least Nick said he would do anything and everything to make sure it was ready.

The sprained ankle had slowed her down, but not Nick. And she'd enjoyed their easy camaraderie as they worked. After a week, she'd hung up her crutches and hobbled around helping him.

They stood in the loft one evening, looking at the box of flooring she'd ordered and discussing which way they'd lay the planks. She turned at the sound of someone coming up the stairs. Mr. Dobbs stood at the top of the stairs, red-faced and slightly out of breath.

"Mr. Dobbs, nice to see you."

"What do you want?" Nick wasn't nearly as polite as she was.

"I heard you were still planning on opening the loft for business by the May Festival."

"Yes, I plan to."

"I didn't see any paperwork for final occupancy permits filed with the planning commission."

"They will be." Annie clenched her teeth. Dobbs could be such a thorn in her side.

"You on the planning commission?" Nick took a step forward then stopped, turned back, and returned to her side.

Maybe he remembered she didn't need him standing up for her. This was her battle. Everything was a battle where Dobbs was concerned. But she was glad he'd stopped and let her handle things.

"Thanks for checking, Mr. Dobbs, but everything is in order. I'm glad you're concerned that I'll be able to open by the May Festival. That's sweet of you to check." She didn't mean a word she said, but whatever, she'd appease the man so he'd leave.

"Make sure it all gets filed in time. We can't have anyone up here if it's not all finalized and legal in time."

She felt Nick stiffen beside her, but he didn't say a word.

"Oh, not to worry. It will all be filed in time." She forced out the words in a cheerful tone of voice.

"I'll be checking." Dobbs turned and headed down the stairs.

Nick stalked to the window. "I don't know why you put up with his... nonsense. He doesn't have anything to do with the planning commission." Nick frowned. "I wonder why his sudden interest in the planning commission."

"I don't know, but he has everything to do with the town. He's on the town council. He can cause trouble. It's easier if you don't rile him." She walked over to stand by him.

"He's an idiot."

"He might be, but he does have power in this town. It's best not to get on his bad side.

Which I'm probably already on because of the river walk brouhaha."

"I can't stand it when people try to abuse their power."

"Nick, I have it under control. We'll be finished in time to get the final inspection. I'm not worried. And I have you to thank for getting me this far along. I'd never have made it on my own. I probably wouldn't have had it finished at all for the tourist season, much less by the May Festival."

"I've enjoyed it. I'd forgotten how much I like doing construction work. It's gratifying to see the project come together." He smiled at her.

That smile of his. The one she reminded herself meant they were just friends.

"How about we take a night off on Monday and go to Antonio's?"

"You don't need to come and work every night. You can take any time off you want."

"No, I didn't mean that. I just thought it would be nice to go have a quick dinner. Besides, I've been craving Antonio's food."

She wasn't sure this was such a good idea. Construction work together? Sure, that was fine. But going out to eat?

"Friends have dinner together." His tone was matter-of-fact.

"Sure. That sounds nice." Why was she being so silly? Of course, friends had dinner together. What difference was it from being with him here at Bookish Cafe or at Antonio's Cantina?

But it *seemed* different.

"Great. Now, let's get this decision made on the flooring." Nick turned and walked over to the planks spread out on the floor.

She followed him across the room, still not sure she'd made the right decision about Monday night.

Nora walked into Bookish Cafe for her planned lunch with Annie. Annie had been so busy with the remodel that they hadn't had much time to see each other. Annie waved from behind the counter and held up one finger.

She wandered over to a book display about Colorado wildflowers and browsed through the pages of the book. She should get a book like this to put out at the lodge. People would probably like to leaf through it or use it to identify flowers around the area.

Annie came up beside her with two boxed up lunches. "I thought we could sit outside on the tables by the river. Might as well enjoy this warm day before that cold front comes through. No snow this time, but I think Colorado can't decide if it wants to let spring actually come this year or not."

They walked outside and settled at a table by the river. Annie looked at the boxes. "Chicken salad or turkey, cheese, and lettuce."

"You choose. Like them both."

Annie slid one over to her.

She opened the box and peeked inside. Chicken salad on a croissant, fruit salad, and a nice-sized brownie. "Perfect choice."

Annie had unwrapped her lunch and was staring at the river.

"Whatcha thinking about?" Nora was pretty sure she knew but figured she'd ask.

"I—what?" Annie blushed. "I was thinking about Nick. He's been such a big help with the remodel. I was wondering when he was going to leave."

"He hasn't said?"

"I think he's still waiting to hear about the research job he wants. It's in Houston."

"You going to be okay when he leaves?"

"I will. We're just friends." Annie's words were a bit too defensive and forceful.

"I am glad he was here to help you with all the carpentry work. I just don't want to see you hurt."

"It's been nice working with him." Annie paused and looked at Nora, then ducked her head. "And we're going to Antonio's on Monday. It's not a big deal though."

Nora just nodded, but she knew Annie *was* going to get hurt. It was clear as day to her even if Annie didn't see it.

Annie was in love with Nick.

And he was leaving.

History was going to repeat itself, and all she could do was be there to pick up the pieces when he left.

CHAPTER 18

Nick grabbed his phone and saw the phone number. Houston area code. He clicked to answer it. "Hello."

"Nick. This is Dr. Middleton. I'm sorry it's taken us so long to get back with you. Things move slowly in the academic world sometimes. Anyway, we would like you to come back for another interview. Are you available to come at the beginning of next week?"

Nick stared out his window. This is what he wanted, right? What he'd been waiting for. "I could make that happen."

"Would Monday work?"

"Yes, it would. I'll get my class here covered. It shouldn't be a problem."

"Great, we look forward to talking to you

again. I'll tell you Nick, you're one of our top choices. I think you'd be a great addition to our research team."

"Thank you."

"So we'll see you on Monday."

"Yes, I'll be there." Nick clicked off the phone. Why wasn't he ecstatic? He'd been waiting for this. The job would be the perfect fit for him. He'd still be able to help kids with cancer. He could still use his knowledge and experience. It was a way to help so many kids.

And help him not feel so guilty for leaving his practice...

And yet, the only thing he could think of is that he'd have to leave Sweet River Falls. He'd have to leave Annie.

But they'd both known the day was coming. The school term was wrapping up. He planned to stay for May Festival and then hopefully go to this job, or if not, he planned to head back to his home in Los Angeles while he looked for work.

He couldn't hide out in Sweet River Falls forever.

Then it hit him. He'd have to cancel his dinner plans with Annie. He raked his hand through his hair. It had taken a bit to convince her to go to Antonio's... and now he had to cancel.

She'd understand. Maybe even be a bit glad. She hadn't been one hundred percent certain that going to dinner was a good idea, but he'd convinced her that friends go to dinner.

He stalked over to the door of his cabin, threw it open, and wandered over to the lake. He watched the wind send gentle ripples across the surface. The sun glistened on the water like someone had scattered a million pieces of broken glass to catch the brilliant rays of light. The hint of pine in the air was now a familiar scent to him once again. The chirping of a bird in the distance and the sight of a hawk swooping over the lake were sights and sounds he'd become accustomed to. It would be hard to give all this up and move back to a busy city. He picked up a smooth rock and tossed it into the lake, skipping it across the surface. Simple pleasures like this. He would miss them.

He turned around and headed back to the cabin. He needed to make his plane reservations and cancel his dinner plans with Annie.

He walked back into the cabin, its simple, comfortable furnishing mocking him. He'd been perfectly content staying here these last few weeks. Hadn't missed his modern, sterile apartment in L.A.

Golden light spilled through the window of Rustic Haven in a welcoming embrace which he resolutely ignored.

With a sigh, he pulled out his phone.

ANNIE STOPPED by the lodge Monday afternoon to see Nora. She was out of sorts today, which was ridiculous. It wasn't a big deal that Nick had cancelled their plans tonight.

Beth's boys came running out of Nora's cabin. "Hi, Annie. We're gonna go to the lodge. Grams says that there are cookies there and we can have some."

"She said we could each have two," Connor corrected.

"You're not the boss of me." Trevor sped off.

The boys raced off down the path to the lodge. Annie knocked once and entered Nora's cabin.

"Annie, there you are. I'm glad you decided to come over. I put on the teapot and sent the boys off for cookies. More so they'd burn off some energy racing over there and back." Nora gave her a quick hug.

"I figured I'd enjoy one of the last few Mondays I'll have off. Once the busy season starts I'll be open every day."

"The busy season keeps us on our toes, doesn't it?" Nora poured two cups of water and grabbed a box of tea.

They settled into their chairs and Annie browsed through the choices of tea, finally deciding on orange pekoe. She dunked her bag into the steaming water.

"I thought you were going to dinner with Nick tonight?" Nora took a tea bag from the wooden box.

"He cancelled. He's gone to Houston. Another interview for the research job."

"Oh."

Annie could see the look on Nora's face clearly said that she thought Annie was making a mistake with Nick. "I know what you're thinking." She let out a sigh. "And you're probably right. I should have kept Nick at arm's length. I will miss him when he's gone. Which is ridiculous."

"Is it?" Nora swirled her tea bag in her cup.

"I just... I can't seem to break the years'

long connection I have with him. You'd think after he left me before, that I'd have been smarter this time. But, you know, there are moments when we're together that everything just seems… right. Which is silly. He's leaving."

She was glad she hadn't told Nora that Nick had kissed her. That was one memory she was keeping to herself. Wrapped up carefully to be relished and taken out later when she felt strong enough to savor it instead of letting it pain her. The kiss was something just between Nick and her, though it was rare to keep something from Nora.

"Sometimes we can't help how we feel." Nora interrupted her thoughts. "We just have to live with the consequence of our emotions."

Annie looked across at her friends. "I've pretty much messed this one up, haven't I?"

"You can't help how your heart reacts. You can hide from it, but if the feeling is still there, then it's still there."

"It is still there…"

"Have you told Nick?"

"No, of course not. He's leaving."

"Maybe you two need to sit down and have a good long talk. At the very least you should tell him how you feel."

"But we agreed we were just friends."

"Is that how you feel? Like he's just a friend?"

Nora was a tough friend to have. She always made her face the truth.

"No… he's not just a friend. I have deeper feelings for him." Annie admitted it for the first time, to herself and to Nora.

Nora reached out and squeezed her hand. "Then talk to him."

CHAPTER 19

Beth rolled up her yoga mat and slipped it into her bag. Sophie leaned against the wall and tugged off her yoga socks and pulled on her shoes.

Beth looked around to make sure she hadn't left anything. "Want to go grab a taco salad at Antonio's?"

"Sounds good. The boys at your Mom's?"

"Yep. Jason is going to run them home for me and said he'd stay if I wasn't there yet. He insisted I ask you to go to dinner. He thinks I work too hard."

"You do," Sophie said matter-of-factly. "But you've always been an overachiever."

"I am not."

"Are so." Sophie grinned. "Like

valedictorian of our high school class, and also head of the yearbook... oh, and class president."

"I... I just like to stay involved."

"Okay, then how about editor of the yearbook in college, head of the student association, and... well, I don't even remember what else." Sophie shook her head, her blonde hair tumbling over her shoulders as she slipped it out of the clip she'd worn for their yoga class.

"I— well, maybe I do volunteer a lot. But like I said, I enjoy staying involved in things."

"That's the understatement of the year." Sophie grabbed her jacket. "Come on. We have two salads waiting for us with our names on them."

They walked to Antonio's and sat at a table near the window. Antonio took their order and Beth leaned back in her seat, sipping on a large glass of water with lemon debating on whether it would be too crazy to do yoga... then have a margarita. It just seemed wrong. No, she'd stick with water. "That was a good yoga session this evening."

"It was. I'm glad we decided to take up yoga. I'm actually getting a bit better with it, I think." Sophie reached for her water. "My balance is still ridiculous, though."

Beth looked up and saw James Weaver making the rounds of the tables, talking to people. "Looks like James is already campaigning for mayor even though he hasn't announced he's running."

"He hasn't formally announced, but everyone knows he's going to." Sophie turned around and looked over to where James was shaking hands with a man at yet another table.

"Even though he's only a few years older than us, for some reason he and Dobbs have become good friends. If he becomes mayor now that Manny had to step down, they'll practically run the town. They'll get everything their way, and only things they agree on will happen. If James had been mayor, I wonder if we'd have gotten the river walk. I like how Sweet River Falls still has its small-town feel, but really, the river walk was such a nice improvement, wasn't it? Dobbs hated that it passed."

"Dobbs does like to have his way. He's been part of the town council for as long as I can remember. It will be a shame if James becomes mayor." Sophie turned back around.

"No one else has said they were going to run." Beth chewed her lip.

Sophie cocked her head. "I don't like the sound of where this is going."

"What? It's not going anywhere. I'm just commenting. Someone should run against him."

"*Someone* should."

Beth laughed. "Oh, don't worry. I don't have time for that."

She watched as James went to yet another table, shaking hands and laughing with the couple sitting there. He might not have declared himself, but it sure looked like he was campaigning.

"Beth... I don't like that look on your face."

She didn't have time to be mayor. She had her boys and her job and the boy's sports and her work at the lodge in the summer. Even thinking about it was crazy.

And she wasn't crazy. Was she?

Sophie just looked at her from across the table and shook her head.

CHAPTER 20

Nick sat on the plane and stared out the window. Fluffy white clouds billowed into pillars alongside the plane. He munched on some kind of snack the stewardess had given him—the exact type of snack hadn't even registered in his mind. They flew past towns nestled in the mountains looking like perfect miniatures below them.

Houston had given him an offer. A good offer. Oh, of course, he wouldn't make as much as he did in private practice, but a good living. And he'd been impressed with their research facilities and excited to get started.

Yet he'd asked them to give him a few days before he gave them his answer. Which was crazy because it was just what he wanted.

But there was Annie to consider now. He couldn't deny it any longer. He had feelings for her. But if he allowed himself to consider his feelings... where did that lead him? He'd be giving up the opportunity to do the research. To possibly help so many kids. It was selfish to give up the opportunity presented to him.

The stewardess came by to collect the plastic glasses and trash, and he put his tray in the upright position as instructed. He closed his eyes as they began their descent into Denver.

He had decisions to make. Hard ones.

Closing his eyes didn't seem to help. The choices danced before him, taunting him.

ANNIE LOOKED at her phone for the hundredth time. She'd expected Nick to text her when he got back, but nothing. She straightened a stack of books and went back to the storeroom to get another bag of coffee beans.

"I've got things here if you want to leave." Lindsey wiped at the counter at the coffee bar. "You've been pacing the store for the last hour or so."

"No... I don't really have anywhere to go.

Just restless today, I guess."

"Well, the offer stands. I could close for you."

"Thanks, Lindsey, but I'm good. I think I'll go up to the loft and get some work done." She headed up the stairs, thankful to escape to the beautiful loft area. It was almost finished. She had the paperwork finished, ready to turn in to request the final inspection. She had just a few trim pieces to put up and do a final look around to make sure everything was set. Might as well do that now.

An order of lounge chairs and small tables was set to be delivered this week. She wanted plenty of seating up here. She'd ordered a long table for one wall and had put in extra electrical outlets for people to use to work and get internet. Everything was just as she'd imagined it. She'd be all set for the May Festival.

She carefully cut the last pieces of trim and trimmed out the last two windows. She stood back and looked at them in satisfaction. Her father had done a good job teaching her the tricks of making perfect corners with trim.

"They look great."

She whirled around at the sound.

Nick stood in the middle of the loft. "Really

good. The whole place looks nice. You did a great job."

"*We* did a great job." She smiled at him. "How did your interview go?" She couldn't stand one more moment of chitchat, she had to know.

"It went... well. They offered me the position."

Annie's heart dropped, but she forced herself to recover and plastered on the most sincere smile she could manage, though she doubted it would fool Nick. "That's great. I'm so happy for you. I know that's what you really want to do. You'll be able to help a lot of kids now."

"I will."

"When do you leave?"

"I leave the end of the first week of May. Right after classes are finished."

A pang of disappointment stabbed her. "You'll miss the May Festival and the grand opening of the loft. That's a shame. You've worked so hard on it."

He scowled. "I know, the timing is terrible. I hate missing the festival. I've been looking forward to it."

"Well, some things are just not meant to be."

She wasn't sure exactly what she was talking about. Wasn't meant to be that Nick went to the May Festival? Wasn't meant to be that there was anything between Nick and her?

Maybe Nora was right, though. She should at least tell him how she felt. Then, he could choose to do what he wanted. Choose his career again. Or maybe—

"Miss Annie. Miss Annie." Connor came racing up the stairs. "Trevor is hurt. A car hit him. We were meeting Momma here. Help me."

Terror gripped Annie's heart. "Nick, come help him." She grabbed Nick's hand and started to hurry after Connor. Nick didn't budge.

"Nick, Trevor needs you." She tugged on Nick's hand.

He stood frozen in place, a look of fear spread across his face. She reached up and slapped his chest with both her fists. "I need you. Please, Nick. It's Beth's son. Please."

His eyes cleared, and he let her pull him down through the store and out onto the street. Annie didn't know what was wrong with Nick or why he hesitated, but she didn't really care right now. All she cared about was Trevor.

Nick raced across the street with Annie. He could see the boy lying in the street. A woman stood beside a car, crying and repeating, "I didn't see him. I didn't see him."

"Get back, let Nick through. He's a doctor." Annie pushed her way through the onlookers.

He followed her and knelt beside the boy. Trevor opened his bright blue eyes, and Nick recognized the look. Pain. The boy was in pain. Those eyes were just like *Billy's* had been. Trevor's pain-filled eyes were more than he could handle. He halted, his hands shaking, and looked at Annie. He shook his head.

"Nick, I don't know what's wrong with you, but you're a doctor. You have the knowledge to help him. Please." She whispered the words next to his ear and grabbed his arm.

He looked back at the boy, drawing on every reserve he had, disgusted with himself for his fear and indecision. This is what he'd become. But he wasn't going to let Annie down. Or the boy. He sucked in a deep breath, trying to get oxygen into his lungs, into his brain, into his hands. Trying to function. "Okay, son. Let me check you out. You okay with that?"

"I hurt everywhere." Trevor let out a sob.

"I'm sure you do. But you'll be fine." What

was he doing making promises like that? He had no idea if the boy would be fine or not. Had he not learned anything from his mistakes?

Trevor closed his eyes.

Relief tiptoed in followed by guilt. It was easier for him to work with Trevor's eyes closed, without his eyes beseeching him to make the pain go away.

After a quick exam, he was certain Trevor's left arm was broken. Even he couldn't doubt that diagnosis. He also had a probable concussion. He'd need a few stitches on a gash on that arm. A siren wailed in the distance. Thank goodness. The EMTs could take it from here. Trevor needed to be checked out thoroughly, and Nick didn't trust his judgment and feared he'd miss something important.

The crowd parted and let the emergency workers through. They knelt beside Trevor.

"He needs to be checked for internal injuries and monitored for a probable concussion. Left arm—radius—appears to be broken. Laceration on his right arm." And they should do any other test they could think of to make sure he was all right. "Don't depend on my assessment, though."

The EMT looked at him. "You a doctor?"

Nick just nodded. But he didn't want them to depend on his findings. They needed to check the boy out thoroughly.

Annie was on her phone. "Yes, I'll ride with him. Meet us at the hospital."

"Nick, can you bring Connor to the hospital? We'll meet Beth and Nora there. I'm going to ride with Trevor in the ambulance so he's not alone."

Annie and Connor came over to stand beside him. The older boy's eyes were wide with fear.

"I told him not to cross in the middle of the street. We're supposed to cross at the corners. He ran out between the cars. I should have stopped him." Tears ran down the boy's face.

"It's not your fault, Connor. Don't even think that." Annie gave him a hug. "Nick?"

Nick kind of heard her, but couldn't make himself respond.

"Nick."

"What?" He tried to pull himself together.

"Will you drive Connor to the hospital?"

"Um, sure." Though why she'd trust him with that responsibility was beyond any sane reasoning. No one should entrust their child to him.

CHAPTER 21

Nora rushed into the waiting room and right up to Annie, grabbing her hands. "Is he okay?"

"I'm not sure. He's in the examining room now. Beth is with him."

Nora raked her hair back from her face. "He has to be okay."

"Nick was there and checked him out. Trevor does have a broken arm. And a pretty bad gash. Maybe a concussion. But Nick told the EMTs to check him for internal injuries and I don't know what all."

"Things can change in an instant, can't they?" Deep lines of worry creased Nora's face, and her eyes clouded with fear.

"He's going to be okay. I feel it. I know it." Annie wrapped her friend in a hug.

"Grams." Connor pushed through the door of the waiting room, raced up to them, and threw himself in Nora's arms.

"Sh. It's okay." Nora held the boy and stroked his head.

"It's all my fault. I should have stopped him. He ran into the street and that lady hit him with her car. It wasn't her fault though. Trev wasn't looking."

"Connor, it's not your fault. It was an accident." Nora put her hands on Connor's shoulders. "You understand? Don't blame yourself."

Nick followed in after Connor. "Any news?"

"Not yet. Beth is back with the doctors."

"Connor, why don't you come sit beside me and we'll wait to hear from your mom?" Nora led Connor over to some chairs in the corner of the waiting room.

"You okay? You're... well, you look really pale." Annie stared at Nick.

"I'm fine. How are you holding up?" He shook his head, dismissing her concern.

"I just want Beth to come out here and say

that Trevor will be okay. You think he'll be okay, right?"

"I… just don't know. I… couldn't say."

Annie didn't like the look on his face. "Do you think something else is wrong?"

"I couldn't make that call. He needs to be checked out."

Beth came out into the waiting room, her face streaked with tears. Nora stood, rushed over, and gathered her daughter in her arms. "Is he okay?"

Beth nodded between sobs. "Yes, he'll be okay. I'm sorry I'm crying. I've just been struggling to hold it together in there for Trevor and I'm just so grateful he's going to be okay."

Annie's heart swelled with relief at the news that Trevor would be okay. She watched while her friend held her daughter and let her cry.

"It's going to be fine. We're all okay," Nora said.

"He has to stay tonight. They want to monitor him for the concussion. He has a cracked rib and they need to set his broken arm. Stitches, too."

"Poor little guy." Nora pushed a lock of hair away from Beth's face. "But the important thing is he'll be okay."

"Yes, that's right. I was just so scared…"

"As any mother would be." Annie walked up and hugged Beth.

"Thanks for riding with him in the ambulance. I couldn't stand to think of him in there alone without a familiar face." Beth's eyes were full of gratitude and relief.

Annie could only imagine what it would be like to hear your child had been in a serious accident. Something she would never experience. "Of course. I'm glad I was there to help."

"I'm going to go back with Trevor, I just wanted you all to know he's going to be okay."

"Mom, I'm so sorry. It's my fault." Connor stood to the side.

Beth walked over and hugged him. "It's not your fault that Trevor didn't follow the rules. He paid a hard price for this lesson, though. I'm just glad it's not worse."

Annie wasn't sure even with all the reassurances that Connor wasn't going to blame himself. Poor kid must have been scared to death to see the car hit his brother.

Beth left to go be with Trevor, and Nora turned to Annie. "Connor and I are going to stay here a while, aren't we kiddo? I called

Jason, and he said he'd get here soon and he can take Connor home with him. You two should go. We'll be fine."

"Are you sure? I can stay with you."

"No, go home and get cleaned up."

She looked down and saw blood on her shirt. "I should probably do that. You promise you'll call if you need anything?"

"I will." Nora led Connor back to the chairs.

Annie turned to Nick. "We should talk."

NICK DROVE Annie back to her cabin. They didn't say a word on the drive even though Annie had said they should talk. He walked her up to her door, and she unlocked it and swung it open.

"Why don't you come in for a few minutes?"

"I—" He really wanted to just run away. A skill he seemed to have perfected.

"Please, let's talk."

He followed her inside. They slipped off their jackets and headed into the kitchen. Annie put on the tea kettle and turned to him.

"Do you want to tell me what happened?"

"What do you mean?" Though he knew exactly what she meant.

"You froze. I needed your help. Trevor needed your help. You're a doctor. But you just froze. There has to be a reason."

Nick looked down at his hands. They both shook, and none of his tricks like clenching his fists or counting to ten did anything to help.

"Nick, what is it?"

"I... I can't."

"He's going to be okay. The doctors said he'd be fine in a little while. Just needs time to heal."

"Or Beth could have just as easily lost him. You never know." He stared at his quivering hands. "I can't... I can't lose another one. I just... *can't.*"

"Nick, what happened? What made you leave Los Angeles?" Annie put her hand on his forearm, but he didn't allow himself to feel any connection.

He closed his eyes, trying to blot out the past, obliterate the memories.

"Talk to me." Annie's low voice pleaded with him.

He sucked in a deep breath, looking for courage. Wondering if he could actually talk about it. If he could talk to anyone about it, it would be Annie. He walked over to her kitchen window and looked out into the darkness. "It was this patient of mine. I mean, I worked in oncology. It came with the job that I'd lose some patients. It was hard with each child I couldn't save. But it was so rewarding when I could cure one of them, or at least put them into remission. That... that was what I lived for in my job." He scrubbed a hand over his face. "But then... this last patient. His name was Billy. William Franklin Evers the Third."

"Like *that* William Evers? The owner of Evers Financial?"

"Exactly like that. His son. He was six years old. A fighter. His eyes... his eyes were that same shade of brilliant blue that Trevor has." His pulse thrummed in his temple. "But nothing anyone had tried would help Billy. I read about this experimental procedure they were doing out of the country and suggested they contact the organizers of the trial. They flew the boy to the research center where they were doing the trial. He seemed to be doing better, and after a while they brought him home."

"But?" Her eyes bore into him. Waiting for him to explain.

"But… he was back in my hospital within weeks and in much worse shape. Maybe some kind of delayed reaction to the treatment, maybe the treatment hadn't really worked. Billy looked at me with his blue eyes so filled with pain, begging me to take his suffering away." Nick swallowed, every tiny detail of the memory etched in his mind. "I couldn't help him. He looked at me with such hope, sure I would save him. But all I could do was try to ease some of this pain."

Annie reached out to touch his face.

"His last words?" Nick closed his eyes. "His last words were 'it's okay Dr. Nick.'"

"Oh, Nick."

Nick opened his eyes. "But it wasn't okay. He died that night. I sat by his side for his last hours on this earth, unable to help him. Unable to give him any more time. Maybe if I hadn't suggested that trial out of the country. Maybe if we'd continued on a more conventional path…"

"It wasn't your fault, Nick. You were trying to help him."

Nick shook his head. "It was my fault. And the torment in his father's eyes as Billy slipped away. I'll never forget it. He wasn't a man to lose at things in life. He blamed himself for taking

Billy over for the trial." Nick raked his hands through his hair. "He shouldn't have blamed himself. He should have blamed me. He trusted me as Billy's doctor. I suggested they try the trial. My decision. My failure. I failed him. I failed Billy."

Nick turned from the window and paced the floor. He felt Annie right beside him. "I can't imagine how it would feel to lose a child. I'm sure his father was torn apart. But Nick, you tried to save the boy."

"But... I couldn't. Then... I started being cautious of making any decisions on treatments for my patients. I was so afraid I'd make another wrong call. I pulled back. Walled off. I just couldn't bear to lose another one." He turned and looked Annie right in the eyes. "So... I left. Ran away to this teaching job. Turned my patients over to my partners. I was no good to them anymore anyway. But I feel terrible I deserted them. But even more terrible that I didn't seem to be able to help them anymore."

"You just needed a break, Nick. You did the right thing."

"Did I? They're all still back there fighting for their lives. I'm here... hiding out. But I'm no good for anyone as a practicing doctor." He walked back over to the window, finally sure of what he had to do. "This is why I'm going to take that research job. For all those patients I left behind. For all the Billys of the world who need us to come up with a cure."

The rightness of his decision settled firmly on his shoulders, and he refused to think about the consequences of that decision.

The fact he'd chosen his career over Annie once again.

ANNIE REACHED out and touched Nick's arm, turning him to face her. Pain seared through his eyes. She reached up and touched his face, and he placed his hand over hers. Without thinking, without caution, she took her hand from his face and wrapped her arms around him, leaning her head against his chest. His heart beat in a riotous rhythm. His strong arms slowly encircled her.

All she could think about was taking away some of his pain, taking away the torment that hovered in his eyes.

"Ah, Annie." His words lingered around her, wrapping her in their desperation and pain.

As she leaned against him, comforting him, she knew what she had to do. What she had to do for Nick. There was no way she was going to tell him her true feelings for him because it was clear he needed to take this research job. In some way, he felt like it would be an atonement for leaving his patients and for what happened to Billy.

There was no way she would ever take that away from him. She may love the man. She *did* love the man. And the fact she loved him so deeply meant she would watch him leave again, let him go follow his career, and never tell him that she loved him.

CHAPTER 22

Beth sat on a bench by the lake at the lodge, watching the boys play. Trevor was recovering quickly as kids do. But she still kept a close eye on both of them. She could barely stand to let them out of her sight. She knew how lucky they'd all been. She knew how an accident could change your life in an instant like it had when Sophie's parents had been killed in that car accident. But her family had been lucky. Trevor would be fine.

Footsteps crunched in the pine needles behind her and she turned to see who was approaching.

"Hey, Sophie."

"Hi." Sophie settled on the bench beside her. "Trevor is looking better."

"He is. I count my blessings every day." She looked over at Trevor standing and watching Connor skip rocks into the lake. "So what brings you out to the lodge?"

"I have some news."

"What's that?"

"It's not good news."

Beth pulled her attention from the boys... kind of... and turned toward Sophie. "What is it?"

"I've heard that the zoning committee might be making some changes to some parcels in Sweet River Falls."

"What parcels?"

"Well, I heard that one of them is on this lake."

"That's strange. This lake is mostly zoned residential, plus it has a few resorts on it, like Mom's, but they are regulated on how many cabins they can have and they all have to be one story. You can only cut so many trees to put in a new cabin. There are a lot of regulations."

"Which is good, because it keeps this place... well, special like it is." Sophie nodded. "But someone wants to change that. I even heard rumors of a request for rezoning for a condo complex."

"They can't do that. Can they? The last thing Lone Elk Lake needs is an overabundance of tourists on it. As it is, you can't even have motorboats on it. Just sailboats, canoes, and rowboats."

"There is also a rumor about the motorboat code on the lake. Plans to change it to allow them."

"I can't see that happening. Who is doing all this?"

"Your friend Mr. Dobbs. I'm pretty sure it's his piece of property right across the lake."

Beth looked across the water, the far lakeside covered in trees with just an occasional house or cabin on the water. "You're kidding me. Well, we have to stop him. It would ruin this peaceful, beautiful lake."

Beth frowned. "So… you know how James Weaver finally announced he's officially running for mayor?"

"I heard that."

"Well, he's on the zoning committee. He'd have to step down from that if he's elected mayor… but he'd appoint the new committee person. And the mayor has the final vote if there's a tie." Beth looked over to check on the boys then turned back to Sophie. "So maybe that's why Dobbs is pushing for Weaver for mayor? Because they're buddies and Weaver can help push through this rezoning?"

"They can't really do it though, can they? A change like that?"

"I don't know, but I'm going to find out." She looked across the peaceful lake. "A big set of condos over there will probably hurt Mom's business, and more than that... it could ruin this lake. We don't need another commercial, gun-your-engines lake around here. It will ruin the... *charm*... of the place."

Beth stood, tugged Sophie to her feet, and called to the boys. "We need to go talk to Mom and let her know what's happening."

CHAPTER 23

Nick packed up his bags and loaded up his rental car. He took one last look around the property. He was going to miss this place. The quiet, the clean air… Annie. The last few weeks had been awkward. He'd helped Annie with a few last touches on the loft, and she'd filed for the final inspection. At least he'd been able to help her with that. There'd been no more meals or visits to her cabin. He'd gone to Bookish Cafe for coffee a few mornings and they'd made small talk. But it had all been so agonizingly tense and uncomfortable.

She knew today was the day he was leaving, and he'd said he was going to stop by her shop on his way out of town, though. He owed her that much.

Nora came walking up the pathway. "I hear you're leaving."

"I am."

She looked at him, and the intensity of her gaze practically seared his skin. She finally shook her head. "I knew this would happen. I knew Annie would get hurt."

"It was the last thing I wanted."

"And yet, it happens again. You leave her. You choose your career over her even after you know how she feels."

He narrowed his eyes. "How she feels? How *does* she feel?"

Nora let out a harrumph. "Nick, I swear. You are the most clueless man I've ever met."

"She said she understands how important this job is to me."

"Of course she did. Would you expect any different from her?" Nora rolled her eyes. "Goodbye, Nick. Don't come back to Sweet River Falls again. Ever. You've done enough damage for a lifetime."

She spun around and headed down the pathway. He slowly climbed into the SUV and put his head on the steering wheel. He'd made a mess of things. He knew he was hurting Annie by leaving. But it was something he had to do. He had to help all those kids. He had to atone for his past mistakes.

Annie understood that even if Nora didn't.

NICK PARKED in front of Bookish Cafe. He sat there staring at the front window of the shop. A pyramid of books adorned one corner of the front display. A bright open sign hung on the door. In another window hung another sign, the first thing that had attracted him to the shop.

Best Coffee in Sweet River Falls.

Annie did have the best coffee in town. Bookish Cafe was welcoming and charming, and he was going to miss popping in here to see Annie. But right now, dread washed over him. He stared at his hands, clutching the steering wheel. He needed to let go of the wheel—it wasn't going to save him—and get out. He needed to go in and say goodbye to Annie.

Slowly, he opened the car door and slid out, looking down at his now-worn cowboy boots. They probably wouldn't see much use at the hospital complex in Houston. He closed the door behind him and resolutely took a step toward the front door.

The door swung open and Trevor hurried out. "Hey, Dr. Nick."

"Hi there, Trevor. Looks like you're feeling better."

"I am. But Mom still doesn't let me do *anything*."

The door popped open again, and Beth and Connor came out. Beth hurried over to Trevor. "What did I say? I asked you to wait for me."

"Sorry, Momma."

Beth looked at him. "I heard you're leaving."

He wasn't sure if he heard recrimination in her voice or she was just stating a fact. "Yes, headed out now."

"Well, safe travels."

"Thanks."

Beth turned away, grabbed Trevor's hand firmly in hers, and headed down the street with her sons. Nick stared at the door to Bookish Cafe again.

Enough of this. Just go inside.

He quickly walked over and entered the shop. Annie looked up from behind the counter as he entered. His heart flipped in his chest.

When would he ever see her again? Of course, he could come visit, but that wouldn't really do either of them any good, would it?

He forced a smile and crossed over to the counter. "Hey, Annie."

She stood quietly and picked up a cloth and started cleaning the countertop. "So, you're headed out now?" Her head was bowed over her work.

"Yes. On my way."

"Well, have a good trip."

"Annie…" He caught her hand and stopped its methodical swiping back and forth on the counter. "I—"

She looked up at him then, with her blue eyes filled with emotions. He could see regret and pain reflected in their depths. His heart squeezed in his chest, and he could barely take a breath.

She finally gave him a small smile. "Goodbye, Nick."

The words rang around him, taunting him, echoing in his mind. "Annie…" But what more was there to say?

He took his hand off of hers. "I'm glad we had this time together. I'm sorry if… if I hurt you again."

"I know, Nick. I know."

His heart numb with a deep ache, he turned and walked to the door. He paused as he opened the door and turned back for one last look at Annie. She raised her hand in a half-wave. He nodded and slipped out the door. Out to his new life, his new career filled with promise. The job he'd wanted.

So why did he feel so incredibly empty and alone?

ANNIE WONDERED how long she'd been standing at the window in the loft, watching the river tumble over the rocks as if hoping it would wash all her pain away.

"I thought I might find you here." Nora walked up beside her.

Annie turned to her friend, not even trying to hide the tears that trailed down her cheeks.

Nora stepped closer and wrapped her in a hug. "I'm so sorry, Annie."

Annie let the warm embrace strengthen her. "It's not like you didn't warn me."

"Well, this is one time I didn't want to be right."

Annie stepped back and swiped at the tears. "I knew this day was coming. I just didn't know it would hurt this much."

"So he came by to say goodbye?"

"He did. Only stayed a minute or so. I mean, there wasn't anything left to say at that point."

"You should have told him how you feel."

"No way I would have stopped him. This job is something he needs to do. I wouldn't do anything to make him feel guilty. He needs to go do this job. He needs it. In some way it will make his decision to quit his private practice make sense to him. He'll still be helping the kids. I can't take that away from him."

Nora didn't look like she was believing a word Annie said.

"It's the only way for him to be happy. To find some peace." Annie took out a tissue and dried the rest of her tears. "I've had my pity party, had my cry. It's all for the best. Now, it's time to get on with my life."

If only her heart could believe her words.

"We all make choices in life. Nick's always seems to be his career over people he loves." Nora scowled.

"He doesn't love me."

Nora looked right at her and rolled her eyes. "Of course he does. Anyone looking at him can see that. He's probably the only one on the planet that doesn't realize it. Well, maybe Nick and *you* are the only ones."

CHAPTER 24

The sun warmed Beth's face as she and Sophie walked down Main Street late in the afternoon. She was so ready for spring weather. They'd hopefully had their last snow, though you could never rule out one last storm in May. For now, she was enjoying the sixty-five-degree weather and only wearing a sweater.

"Wonder what's going on there." Sophie pointed to the larger bricked area that led to the river walk. "That's quite a crowd."

They hurried up the street and stood near the back of the crowd. James Weaver stood on the small platform by the fountain. "I just want to formally announce that I'm running for Mayor in our special election. I'm sorry Manny's health took a bad turn and he had to step down, but I assure you I'm ready to take over and keep everything running smoothly. I turned in the official paperwork today."

Beth clasped her purse tightly and watched as Dobbs wound his way through the crowd.

Clapping broke out in the crowd, then Mr. Dobbs stepped up beside James. "Well, it looks like you're going to have the job." He clapped James on the back. "Since you're the only one running."

The crowd laughed.

"But I'm sure you'll do a fine job for us."

"Excuse me." Beth pushed through the crowd.

"Hey, little lady. Did you come to congratulate Mr. Weaver?"

Beth bristled at Dobbs's words and his tone, even more sure of herself now. "No... actually..." She stepped up beside the men and opened her purse. "I've filled out the paperwork to run for mayor, too. I'm on my way right now to turn it in to city hall."

"What?" Dobbs's face grew redder and redder. "But you're not qualified."

"I guess we'll let the voters decide that, won't we?" Beth turned to the crowd. "I'll be sure to let you know my platform and ideas for the town. Feel free to stop me and ask questions any time you see me." She turned to James. "May the best person win."

She held out her hand and wasn't sure that James was going to shake. He finally stuck out his hand and shook hers quickly, drawing it back immediately as if he couldn't bear to be seen with her. She gave him her best dazzling smile, then waved to the crowd. She climbed off the platform and walked over to where Sophie stood at the edge of the courtyard.

"Are you crazy?" Sophie shook her head.

"Probably."

Sophie grinned. "Well, yes you are crazy, but I'm with you one hundred percent. I'll be your campaign manager. I'll do anything to help you. We have to stop them."

ANNIE KEPT as busy as possible so she didn't have time to think about Nick, not that it was really working. She thought about him all the time. Every fiber of her being missed him. His smile. His laugh. The way he teased her. She missed having him beside her as she finished up things with the loft.

She looked around the loft, now filled with furnishings. It did look inviting, and she was pleased how it all had turned out. Except that Nick wasn't up here with her…

She shoved the thoughts aside and scooted a chair next to the long pine workstation along the far wall.

Annie looked up, surprised to see James Weaver at the top of the stairs to the loft. "Mr. Weaver, hi."

"Hello, Annie."

"Can I help you?"

"I've come to do the final inspection on the loft."

Annie frowned. Mr. Weaver wasn't the normal inspector. "I thought Henry did the inspections."

"He's out of town. I'm also certified as an inspector, so I fill in when he's not available." Mr. Weaver crossed into the center of the loft, looking around. He held a clipboard in his hands and made notes as he carefully inspected each area.

"I'm sure you'll find everything in order. I followed the approved plans exactly."

"Hm." He wandered over to the table along the wall. He took out a tape measure and measured between the many outlets along the wall. He measured between the outlets under the windows and jotted down a note.

He took more measurements and asked to see the circuit board. Annie felt an uneasiness surround her the longer the man wandered around the loft.

He scribbled some more on his clipboard and handed her a paper. "These things don't meet code. You can correct them and reapply for another inspection."

She looked at the paper in amazement. "I don't understand. I turned in the plans. These are things that were never corrected on my original set of plans. They were never mentioned."

"Can't speak to that. I'm just going by what I see and the codes." He turned to walk away but paused. "Shame it looks like you won't be able to open up by this weekend's May Festival. With Henry out of town, I'm really booked with inspections. Should be able to get to you sometime next week for a reinspection." With that, he headed down the stairs, and Annie sank onto a chair, letting the paper fall to the ground.

CHAPTER 25

Nick walked down the sterile hall of the hospital on his way to the research wing. The familiarity of walking the halls, wearing a white coat, the bustle of activity on the floor— all this should feel right to him. Only it didn't feel right, not at all. He turned the corner, headed to the elevator, and punched the up button.

Instead of being excited to be going to work, excited about being in on some cutting-edge research, he was just numb. He thought the excitement of meeting new colleagues and reviewing the research to get caught up to speed would keep him buried in work, unable to think about Annie. So far his plan hadn't worked. She was on his mind every single minute of every day.

And the nights.

The nights were the worst.

Alone in his temporary, furnished-in-commercial-plainness apartment.

The elevator opened, and an older couple stood in the doorway. They held hands, and the man was looking at the woman like she was the center of his universe. They looked up at him and smiled.

"Good morning." The man nodded at Nick.

"Morning."

"It is a good morning. We're headed home. They gave me my walking papers. But first, my husband is going to take me for a nice piece of peach pie."

"Whatever you want, dear. Just glad to be taking you home with me." The man kissed her on her forehead, and she broke into a brilliant, just-for-her-husband smile.

The couple walked out of the elevator, and Nick stood and watched them as they continued down the hallway, perfectly in sync, holding hands. The man leaned closer and said something to his wife, and her delighted laugh rang out down the hallway.

And suddenly he knew what he wanted. What he needed. He wanted what those two had and so much more.

And none of it involved research in Houston, far away from Sweet River Falls.

NICK PULLED into town and searched for a parking spot on Main Street. No luck. The town was bustling with people here for the May Festival. Bright banners were strung across Main Street. It was still early, but doors to the shops were wide open, and people milled down the sidewalk.

He pulled down a side street and found a spot in a gravel parking lot. He jumped out of the car, eager to be here for Annie's grand opening of the loft. He hurried up the side street and ran into Jason at the corner.

"Nick. Didn't expect to see you here."

"Me either. I've been pretty much the fool. But I'm over that now." He grinned at Jason. "I came to see Annie's grand opening."

"Well, that isn't happening."

"What do you mean?" He frowned.

"Oh, it seems that we've managed to rile a

few people in town. Mainly James Weaver and Old Man Dobbs. Weaver did the final inspection and didn't pass the loft. Said he didn't have time to reinspect it until after the weekend."

"Why would he be inspecting it? Isn't Henry still the inspector?"

"He is, but it seems he took the week off. Gone off fishing somewhere. And evidently James inspects when Henry is gone."

"So what does James have to gain by not passing it?"

"A favor to Dobbs? Payback for winning the town over to put in the river walk? Or maybe because my sister decided to run against Weaver in the mayoral election?"

"She did? Good for her." Nick looked down the street. "Annie must be so disappointed."

"She is. And my mom is madder than a wet hen. Last I saw, she was off to find Dobbs and give him an earful."

"You say Henry is off fishing?"

"Yep. So I'm afraid Annie will have to postpone the grand opening until after she can get all the code things sorted out. She fixed the bogus things on Weaver's list, but he insists he can't reinspect until next week sometime."

"We'll see about that." Nick spun around and headed back to his car. There was no way he was going to let Annie's big day be spoiled. He knew she liked to solve her own problems, but he wasn't going to let some cranky, vindictive old man ruin Annie's plans.

ANNIE AND NORA stood in Bookish Cafe. Annie watched as people walked down the street. Many came in for coffee and to browse the books, but as the shop filled up, more people peeked in and wandered off down the street. She sure could have used the extra space today.

"I'm sorry, Annie." Nora squeezed her hand. "Dobbs is a mean-spirited old man."

"Well, he got his revenge, didn't he? He's still so angry about the river walk."

"And angry that Beth is running against Weaver for mayor. I think she's crazy for running, but what can I say? She wants to try and stop Dobbs from being able to sell his property on Lone Elk Lake. If Weaver wins, it's a certainty that we'll have a stiff fight to keep it from happening."

"Dobbs is a troublemaker, that's for sure."

As disappointed as she was, Annie shrugged. "Well, there's nothing I can do. I'll just have to make the best of it."

She heard a commotion outside the door to the shop and headed over to see what was going on. She froze in place as she saw him.

"Nick." She whispered his name.

"Hey, Annie." He stood with a big grin on his face, a fistful of balloons, and a big chalkboard easel with the words Grand Opening scrawled across the sign.

"What are you doing here? And there isn't a grand opening. The loft didn't pass."

Henry walked up to them. "Sure it did." He thrust a paper at her. "I was just up there checking. Everything is fine."

"How? I mean, I thought you were out of town." How did he get up there without her seeing him? She must have missed him in the crowd of people.

"I was. Fishing. But Nick here used to be a fishing buddy of mine. He knew where to find me. Convinced me to come back to town and check out the loft. Fishing was lousy today anyway." Henry winked. "Besides, Nick is a pretty persuasive guy."

Annie stood there, dazed, as Nora walked

up beside her. "You okay—" Nora looked up and spotted Nick. "What's *he* doing here?"

"Came for Annie's grand opening now that Henry has passed everything." Nick carefully set up the sign by the door and attached the balloons. "Oh, and I've ordered dozens of cupcakes that will be delivered from Mountain Grove within the next hour that you can give away to your patrons."

Dobbs came hurrying up the street. "Hey, you can't put up that sign. She can't open. Weaver didn't pass the loft."

Henry stepped up to Dobbs. "But I did. Those were ridiculous violations anyway. Not really true ones. But she did everything on Weaver's list, so she's all set now."

"You can't do that."

"Of course I can. I'm the inspector. No law says I can't inspect on a beautiful Saturday like this one."

"But…" Dobbs sputtered.

"It's a done deal," Henry assured him.

Dobbs turned and stalked away, muttering under his breath.

Annie turned to Nick. "But what are you *doing* here?" She couldn't quite keep up with all that was happening.

"I'm here to tell you that I'm a fool. That I've made a terrible mistake." He reached out and took her hand in his. "I'm here to ask you to forgive me."

"I—" Her heart pounded as she tried to keep the world from spinning out of control.

"I'm here to stay if you'll have me. And by stay, I mean forever. I want to marry you, Annie."

The breath whooshed out of her lungs, and she heard Nora gasp behind her.

Nick dropped to one knee on the sidewalk. "Annie, will you marry me? I love you. Always have, always will."

Nora poked her in the back. "Answer the man."

"I…" She broke into a huge smile and every cell of her being felt like it could explode with happiness. "I love you too. And, yes, I'll marry you."

Nick jumped to his feet and let out a whoop. He scooped her up and whirled her around. When he finally set her back on the sidewalk, he leaned down and kissed her. The kiss that she'd waited for and longed for.

The crowd around them started clapping,

and Annie felt a warm blush creep over her cheeks.

"We should probably go turn on those lights upstairs and open up the loft." Nora stood grinning by the door, then answered herself. "Yes, I think *I* will go do that. Annie's a little busy right now."

"I'll help you. Then I think I'll get one of those best-in-Sweet-River-Falls cups of coffee. Nora, you care to join me?" Henry held open the door.

"Sure." Henry and Nora went inside, leaving Annie standing facing Nick while people streamed past them and into Bookish Cafe.

Annie looked up at Nick. "I thought I'd lost you forever."

"Not a chance." He kissed her again, then pulled back. "Though next time I'm being a fool, you might want to clue me in."

She smiled up at him. "I will."

"I guess getting married tomorrow would be too soon?" Nick raised an eyebrow.

"Now, that is foolish, Nick." Annie nodded gravely. "I think it will take me at least a week to pull it off."

"Whoop!" Nick scooped her up and swung her around again. "A week? I don't doubt you will. I love you, Annie. We're going to be so happy."

She touched his cheek, tears threatening the corners of her eyes. "I'm already happier than anyone else in the whole world."

"Me too, my love. Me too." And he kissed her again.

CHAPTER 26

A*lmost* true to her word, Annie quickly planned the wedding. It did take her two weeks to pull it off, though, with a lot of help from Nora.

Nora stood beside her friend at the gazebo by the lake at Sweet River Lodge. Annie wore a simple white dress and held a bouquet of light blue hydrangeas. She'd never looked lovelier. Annie's eyes glistened with tears as she stood beside Nick and recited her vows.

Nick wore an adorably smitten look on his face, which is what Nora needed to see. She hoped that now that Annie and Nick had found each other again, their lives would be blessed with love and happiness.

"I now pronounce you husband and wife." The minister smiled at the couple.

Nick leaned down, brushed away a tear from Annie's face, and kissed her gently. "I love you."

Nora could just hear Nick's whispered words to his bride.

"I love you, too." Annie beamed as she touched Nick's face in a gesture so very gentle and intimate.

Nick took Annie's hand in his, and they turned and stepped off the gazebo and down the aisle strewn with flower petals. Their friends stood and clapped and cheered.

Nora fought back her own tears. She wanted nothing more than to see her friend happy. She couldn't help but remember her own wedding so many years ago on the shore of this very same lake. How life has a way of throwing curves and laughing at a person's well laid out plans. A familiar ache filled her heart as she thought of her husband, taken from her at way too young an age. She glanced up at the fluffy cloud covered sky and murmured, "I miss you. Always."

A great blue heron swooped past along the edge of Lone Elk Lake. She smiled. Her husband's favorite bird. One always seemed to make an appearance when she needed it.

She stepped off the gazebo and headed after her friend, content in the knowledge that Annie had discovered true love and happiness, even if it had taken her decades to find it.

Love was funny like that. You just never knew when it would find you.

Dear Reader,

I hope you enjoyed Annie's story. Interested in reading more stories set in the town of Sweet River Falls? Read Beth's story in book two, *A Memory to Cherish*.

The one thing Beth Cassidy doesn't plan on is Mac McKenna showing up in Sweet River Falls. At exactly the wrong time…

Mac moved away from Sweet River Falls and has no desire to have anything to do with the town that always considered him an outsider, but he can't fight his growing attraction for the woman trying to overcome her own reputation in town.

But Mac seems to be *right there* every time

something goes wrong. The cops and the town will never believe he's innocent.

Mac vows to wipe the dust of Sweet River Falls from his boots, and leave the town far, far behind. For good this time. He means it.

Mac leaving for good is probably for the best. Beth is sure of it. Pretty sure…

Will Beth and Mac find a way to have more than just A Memory to Cherish?

Want to be the first to know about exclusive promotions, news, giveaways, and new releases? Sign up for my newsletter at my website: kaycorrell.com

OR JOIN my reader group on Facebook.

https://www.facebook.com/groups/KayCorrell/

They're always helping me name my characters, see my covers first, and we just generally have a good time.

As always, thanks for reading my stories. I truly appreciate all my readers.

Thank you and happy reading!

THANK YOU for reading my story. I hope you enjoyed it. Sign up for my newsletter to be updated with information on new releases, promotions, give-aways, and newsletter-only surprises. The signup is at my website, kaycorrell.com.

Reviews help other readers find new books. I always appreciate when my readers take time to leave an honest review.

I love to hear from my readers. Feel free to contact me at authorcontact@kaycorrell.com

COMFORT CROSSING ~ THE SERIES

The Shop on Main - Book One

The Memory Box - Book Two

The Christmas Cottage - A Holiday Novella (Book 2.5)

The Letter - Book Three

The Christmas Scarf - A Holiday Novella (Book 3.5)

The Magnolia Cafe - Book Four

The Unexpected Wedding - Book Five

The Wedding in the Grove (crossover short story between series - Josephine and Paul from The Letter.)

LIGHTHOUSE POINT ~ THE SERIES

Wish Upon a Shell - Book One

Wedding on the Beach - Book Two

Love at the Lighthouse - Book Three

Cottage near the Point - Book Four

Return to the Island - Book Five

Bungalow by the Bay - Book Six

CHARMING INN ~ Return to Lighthouse Point

One Simple Wish - Book One

Two of a Kind - Book Two

Three Little Things - Book Three

Four Short Weeks - Book Four

Five Years or So - Book Five

Six Hours Away - Book Six

SWEET RIVER ~ THE SERIES

A Dream to Believe in - Book One

A Memory to Cherish - Book Two

A Song to Remember - Book Three

A Time to Forgive - Book Four

A Summer of Secrets - Book Five

A Moment in the Moonlight - Book Six

INDIGO BAY ~ Save by getting Kay's complete collection of stories previously published separately in the multi-author Indigo Bay series. The three stories are all interconnected.

Sweet Days by the Bay

Or buy them separately:

Sweet Sunrise - Book Three

Sweet Holiday Memories - A short holiday story

Sweet Starlight - Book Nine

ABOUT THE AUTHOR

Kay writes sweet, heartwarming stories that are a cross between women's fiction and contemporary romance. She is known for her charming small towns, quirky townsfolk, and enduring strong friendships between the women in her books.

Kay lives in the Midwest of the U.S. and can often be found out and about with her camera, taking a myriad of photographs which she likes to incorporate into her book covers. When not lost in her writing or photography, she can be found spending time with her ever-supportive husband, knitting, or playing with her puppies —two cavaliers and one naughty but adorable Australian shepherd. Kay and her husband also love to travel. When it comes to vacation time, she is torn between a nice trip to the beach or the mountains—but the mountains only get considered in the summer—she swears she's allergic to snow.

Learn more about Kay and her books at kaycorrell.com

While you're there, sign up for her newsletter to hear about new releases, sales, and giveaways.

WHERE TO FIND ME:
kaycorrell.com
authorcontact@kaycorrell.com

Join my Facebook Reader Group. We have lots of fun and you'll hear about sales and new releases first!
https://www.facebook.com/groups/KayCorrell/

facebook.com/KayCorrellAuthor

instagram.com/kaycorrell

pinterest.com/kaycorrellauthor

amazon.com/author/kaycorrell

bookbub.com/authors/kay-correll